Ann M.
Greenseth

According to Lu

I dedicate this work to all
who find the courage to ask for help,
and to all who have the audacity to provide it.

Award-winning Finalist in the Fiction: Inspirational and Fiction: Novella categories of the 2020 International Book Awards

ISBN: 978-1-7348169-0-7

Cover artwork by:
Myimagine/Shutterstock.com
Ksenia Lada/Shutterstock.com
Internal artwork by:
Ksenia Lada/Shutterstock.com
Cover and internal artwork were purchased from Shutterstock (www.shutterstock.com)

Cover design by: Ann M. Greenseth

Printed in the United States of America

According to Lu

Ann M. Greenseth

My dear Thea,

I enclose the journal entries I collected during my extended journey. These words and messages are from reliable witness. They are testaments to the Sacred in each of us; as such, you may be assured of the truths they divulge. I endeavored to retain the voice of each narrator, and pray I have done them justice.

I cherish each one, even as I treasure the whole. I believe you will, too.

Though these pages have a beginning and an end, the narrative continues.

Blessings,

Lu

Promise 1

With both hands, she placed the cup carefully on the table, as if she thought it might break. Perhaps she feared the sound of ceramic on wood would cause her thoughts to collide and explode into a million sharp, tiny shards.

Bezla folded her arms in front of her and rested her forearms on the table, staring into the dark liquid in the cup.

Slowly, she replayed in her mind the series of events, letting them blend from one scene into another. Sorrow. Years of it. And then… news. A baby. After all these years. After all her prayers. A baby.

Intense joy flooded her senses, and then, just as intensely, fear charged in. But the latter was a small cloud of dust that she brushed away, leaving behind the joy, calmer now, uplifting, soaring. But not setting her heart racing. No, that had been the fear. With that gone, there was a only joyous gravity.

Then came the journey home with the news.

In her mind, angels sang the news throughout the heavens.

Bezla would never forget the look in Shem's eyes. Her husband, who was notably not the most communicative of men, retreated into a deeper silence. His eyes glazed. She knew he had heard, but she only knew because of long years of proximity. No one else would have guessed; they would have told her to say it again, since he obviously hadn't heard her the first time.

He had heard.

She might have expected his reaction—or lack thereof—would crush her. Or startle, or at least tarnish her joy, blow the dust of fear and defeat back onto her heart.

But her joy persisted, undiminished.

The quiet of the joy deepened when she heard of her sister's daughter, and the news of her joy. For that is how she viewed it. Again, Bezla daydreamed, hearing blessed music with the words her young niece spoke. And she spoke with quiet joy. She took her niece's hands in her own small hands, and helped her kinswoman to brush away the cloud of fear, to feel only the joy.

And the baby's kick, at the sound of their laughter. Clearly the little one was feeding off their joy. They knew the giddiness of life making itself known in Bezla, still but a promise in her niece. Women's voices raised together in laughter, in joy at life and life-bearing, in songs that the heavens hear and take delight in hearing.

Startled by a spasm of muscle, and attendant pain, the scenes from the past disconnected like clouds parting. The sun shone through. It was time.

The fear re-appeared, but just as quickly dissipated. She rose from the table to seek assistance.

Pain, but only physical, followed. And more. And more. In between, she saw again bits of the dreamy landscape of the past several months—moments of angels' laughter, scraps of music, smiles and tears—punctuated by the spasms.

And then the baby was in her arms. The joy Bezla felt, as compared to the day when she carried her news home, as compared with the days with her niece and the days since, was tenfold.

She gazed into the wizened face, and she knew that someone of import had just entered the world. And not just her world. The world at large. And her niece's world, too. She didn't understand the feelings, couldn't see through the haze that drifted around her thoughts, but the knowledge was somehow there.

The baby opened her eyes. All haze drifted away and Bezla smiled. The joy. "My joy," she whispered, "my delight." The baby gurgled. A strong-voiced gurgle. She laughed softly at the sound her baby made.

"Delah, you have a strong voice," she murmured.

"My daughter." Her husband's voice hovered outside her happiness. Slowly, she let Shem in and delighted in both their presences.

"Our daughter," she said softly.

He smiled.

Promise  2

I knew it, all along. I knew it. Not in a way I could show you. Or anyone. But I knew.

First, the dreams. So real. So strange. They frightened me. I tried to tell, but couldn't. They kept coming. It's as if, like, I got used to 'em. They made more sense. I… well, I began to look forward to 'em.

My Gran used to say, Briel, dreams, the good ones, are angels visiting you. Then, my angel visited me. My angel.

Now, there is life in me. See, words don't work. I can't really tell you what I mean. Words, they don't work.

But the life is there, words or no words, it's there. In me.

Oh, I was so frightened. So… frightened. No, they said. No, don't do it. You so young. Don't. Your life over before it's begun. Can't be a mother. Talk, talk. More words. Foul words. That's it. Foul.

I was startin' to listen. I was. Really listen. And then, the angel.

That's all it took. That's all. You can't understand, but it was, well, like a light that is suddenly there. There's still darkness, in the corners. But, if you pay attention, really pay attention, you see the light, glowing, bright, warm, gentle, and nothing else matters. Not all the words or shadows in the world matter.

Their words, they bring on the darkness.

All but one. She took my hands, looked into my eyes, she said no words, and I didn't either, and she knew.

I know it was hard. I know it. When all the words are darkness and the only light is silence, it's hard. I'm not used to it, to silence. I wasn't, that is. But I got used to it. I got so that all I could hear was the silence.

It was then I could feel the heartbeat, inside of my own. Pit-pat. There, soft and steady.

She took my hand, and I swear she could hear the heartbeat, too. She smiled, I smiled. And I knew. The words of darkness could not reach me. Oh, they tried and tried. I may have weakened a bit at times, but then I would hear that pit-pat. And then feel the movement, below my ribs. A quick jab from inside to remember the light. A reminder, that's what it was.

I was alone, surrounded by those words of darkness, but I didn't feel alone. Know what I mean?

No, how could you?

Unless you know. You've seen that light, small, but beating back the darkness. Heard that pit-pat, so soft, but filling the universe, known the feelings that make the light, still the noises, all but the ones that matter, pit-pat. Felt the movement, too small for every day but so large it makes a moment.

That movement. It is my life. I don't think I was really alive before. How do I find words to say that? To make anyone understand? I can't.

I don't have to. That's not my job. It's my baby's.

See? She something. She something that we don't know yet. She someone we haven' never seen. She somebody we can never expect, and always want to be there, but don't believe she can. We hope for, and fear.

That's what she is.

That's why I choose her. That's why she chose me. That's the truth. But they don't understand. They won't. They chose not to. She chose me.

I am blessed. My Gran used to say that about me. Briel, she said, you are blessed. She was right. She just don't know why. Or how right she is. I am blessed.

I don't understand blessings. It don't matter. I don't even have to try no more.

She's growing. She understands. She'll understand for me. And I just don't need anything else.

Gift  1

Babies are born every day. That's what I told Kahbe. And then suggested he get back to work. Who can understand him? That husband of mine. He sits and chatters when there is so much work to do. Malak, he says, it's good for business. What the customers want, expect. Bah! I said in response.

With all the people traveling to the area, we are going to have more and more guests staying here. More and more work to do.

Anyway, that's what I told him. Babies, babies. Big deal. Not like one's never been born here before, heaven knows. Not that we want that to happen here. But it has.

But for it all to happen so quietly. The woman, so quiet you'd hardly notice her. Except, of course, for that big load she carried. High, too. Gonna be a girl, I thought when I saw her. Then forgot about them. There was so much to do. There's always so much to do.

It was long past dark, I remember that. Long past. I thought everyone had finally settled down. I sat down, wanting to put my feet up and not worry about anything. Gonna be a long week, I remember thinking.

And I heard it. A baby's cry. I knew right then. I don't even remember standing up and moving, but there I was. Out in the darkness. I found them in the dark. A small light glowing there steadily.

I stood there. It hadn't really been a cry, I recall thinking. More like a, well, an announcement. Here I am. I know, I know. I'm just telling you how it felt, you know? 'Course it felt strange. I think I must have stood there a long time. I think so.

I didn't want to disturb them, but, well, a good host sees to her guests, right? I'm saying this now, so you understand. But I didn't really think about disturbing or not disturbing them. I wasn't thinking at all. Not right then. I didn't think about being a host, good or bad.

A baby. A girl. Just like I thought. Born every day, right? Several right under my nose. But, well, this was different.

Oh, why bother. I can't explain. Ten fingers, ten toes, two arms, two legs. A baby. Like any other baby. Right?

People came to see. Other people. Not just me. Like we'd all been called. Though no one made a sound. Not that momma, not that baby.

Her little fists waved in the air. But she made no sound.

It was quiet. Not an uneasy quiet. Not uneasy, like I'm feeling right now, trying to tell you. No. Not uneasy. Welcome. Like we were welcome. Like we were… expected. No, not like any other feeling I ever had.

I always wanted to make people feel welcome like that. Always. But I just didn't really know it 'til then.

How can a baby teach you that?

Well, I'll tell you, I've changed my mind 'bout that. I'm beginning to believe babies can teach us anything we need to know. Teach exactly what we need to know, right there, right then.

It's like we know everything then, and then give up what we know. Give it up because we think we have to. Or, are told we have to? We believe others instead of ourselves. Adults instead of children. Or babies. There's nothing they don't know. Nothing!

I know, you don't believe me. I know, I'm strange, you say. But I know that I saw something there that night. Felt something. Something real. Right there with that quiet momma, and that quiet little baby.

I'd like to tell Kahbe, that husband of mine, the truth. But I tell him to go back to work. That's what I do. Well, sometimes, I do. That's all he can understand.

But I try. Each day I try. To welcome people. Really welcome them.

And sometimes, just sometimes, I sit and chat with them. And sometimes, when he sits there and jokes with them, I just walk on by. Without saying a word. Welcome them, I tell myself and silently tell him.

Like the little baby.

Gift  2

I'd felt that tingling sensation in my palms only once before. It was so powerful, the feeling that came with it. It set me on a path I had not expected.

One other time, that is all. Oh, I've "felt" things since that first time – enough to advise. Or, to keep from advising.

That first time, I was twelve years old. I held my mother's hand. We were in a crowd. I remember being distracted by one of the vendors. I can't really remember what it was he was selling, except it sparked in the sun. And that was what caught my eye.

I wanted to see it, and tried to through the milling crowd. I reached up to take my mother's hand again. I was intent on pulling her there, to that stall, to show her the source of light. My hand reached up and my fingers closed on... it's hard to describe. They were fingers, but old and ropy and knuckly – not my mother's hand.

The tingling burst in my palms and I grasped that hand so tightly. I stared up, but the sunlight blinded me. I could barely make out a head towering above me.

And I said strange things. I didn't cry for my mother. I didn't let go of the hand. I loosened my hold, but did not let go. I told the woman, the old woman I had grasped, that her son was calling for her, that her daughter was dancing in moonlight, that her husband waited for her, with laughter and tears.

I told her that her sister knew pain no more and her mother waited for her. I told her that she would hear rain in the morning, and see the sun shine through.

My mother found me then, and dragged me away, but only after prying my fingers from the old woman's hands and from her arm. My mother mumbled words to the woman. I couldn't understand. All I could think about was that I didn't want the feeling, the tingling, to go away. But it drained out of my hands.

My mother knew the old woman and her family. So she told me, some time later. But that next day, the day after that strange day in the market, she said nothing. She looked at me strangely.

We heard, or she did, that the old woman died that next morning. After it rained. And the sun broke through the clouds. My mother said nothing more of it. Not then.

After a time, most people forgot about that strange day. You see, so many people were in the market that day and witnessed my revelations. They knew my mother. And knew the old woman. Knew her family. They grew used to me again after that, but never treated me quite the same. My mother they grew close to again. But all remained wary of me.

Three years later, I was fifteen. I'd had feelings about people, most of which I kept to myself. I tried and succeeded in keeping much of it to myself. But, strangely, I was lonely. I knew it was because of that day, and of seeing what I had seen, and speaking what I had spoken.

So, I asked my mother. For the first time in a long, long time, she stopped bustling around the house. Sit, she said, and then sat down opposite me. Nah, my dear daughter, she began. She told me that the old woman's son and daughter, twins, had died young of a strange illness, and that her son had been weak toward the end, calling her name. But her daughter had smiled, told her she was going to dance, and then died. That her husband had died also, very recently, and that they'd been very close. That the old woman's sister had died that morning I'd grasped her hand, after a long illness. And that the old woman told her she'd had a dream, where her mother smiled at her and said, Daughter, I am waiting for you.

Then she stopped speaking and simply looked at me. "Nah," she stated, "it is a gift." But her tone of voice said it was not.

Since then, that tingling never re-occurred, not like that market day. Until today. So many years later.

The child knew. She knew I saw visions of wellsprings and swords, of things ancient and new, of beginnings and of endings. I grasped her tiny hands, knew they were tingling as mine were, and spoke words of blessing that came to me, just as the words had so long before, words for all to hear.

But what I saw beyond her shining eyes, only I know. And only she knows. No one else.

I am very old. I knew these things when I was quite young. And I know them again, now that I am old. Ancient, healing, powerful, this knowledge.

My mother, long ago, said it was a gift. Forgive me, mother, because I believe you only now.

Resolution 1

Dayane stood, triumph glowing, shining from her eyes. She felt the power, so vast it was evaporating through her skin, blending into the air around her, oozing from her soles into the shadows at her feet. Triumph, in simply watching that woman being dragged away in chains. Justified. Righteous. Filled with contempt.

It was all worth it, she told herself. It was worth the betrayal—of her friends, her infidel of a husband. Even, she asserted, her daughter.

Just to observe her in chains.

To know she is imprisoned. And a sentence to be carried out soon.

After all, it wasn't just herself that woman had dared to defy. The troublemaker had denounced my own husband, Dayane mused. Granted, he deserved criticism. But not by one so poor, so unknown, so lesser.

The chains. Ah, the chains. She lifted her head again, staring after the prisoner, though she and her captors and guards were long gone.

Then it struck her. The room was empty, hollow. Nothing was shining, only shadowed. She was suddenly quite afraid to move, fearful of the scraping sounds she knew her sandals would make on the polished floor, how the scratching would echo and re-echo in the emptiness. And grow louder. Accentuating the silence.

Fear gripped Dayane, and wrung at her bones. She stood, frozen, afraid of hearing her own joints creaking inside her skin if she dared to move.

Then, her own breathing seemed to sound like a tempest howling through a valley, rasping in and out of her lungs.

She uttered a cry, and clapped her hands together, as if in spasm. Echoes upon echoes. The flood of fear ebbed with the sounds and echoes of the sounds, but it did not disappear. Her breathing steadied.

Then, the horror.

Dayane knew, in a sudden flash of insight, that her husband would not come here. Nor her daughter. Those she betrayed. Never. Never again. Servants only. Guests, if she invited them. But no one else.

She attempted to conjure the feelings of triumph. She closed her eyes and willed them to come back. There was nothing, at first.

She gasped and her eyes flew open. She could see the prisoner's eyes. And her daughter's eyes. Betrayed. Confused. Disbelieving and then, worse, believing. Quickly, she blinked her eyes trying to brush away the images. Then she stared. I dare not close them again, she thought.

She bellowed for her servants. They cowered before her, ran to do her bidding. Dayane raged, chastised, and screamed at imagined error. Yet the eyes were still there, in front of her or behind her own eyelids, staring at her, making her see.

Where was the triumph? she thought. The righteousness? So fleeting.

She realized. She gasped.

Who is my enemy now?

Water. It is remarkable. Gives life, cleanses. It is fun to play in.

It falls from heights, as waterfalls or rain—and makes a most pleasant variety of sounds.

It is patient. It carves at rocks and soils, sculpting endlessly, making its own beds.

It is generous, feeding and feeding itself and those of its kind, its kin—the streams, the rivers, the lakes, the sea.

It is beauty, in itself and reflecting. It is blue, crystal clear, or gray and billowing and stormy, reflecting the sky and the weather. It sings. It blesses. It rumbles and tumbles.

And to think I never really saw it before, understood its value, uses, gifts. I saw only the necessities—the need to haul buckets of it from its source to the house, to use it when cooking, to wash floors and clothes, to quench a thirst.

I see these things now, but I cannot say them. I dare not. No one would listen. No one hears me. I dare not.

But it sings to me. It sings and whispers as I fry the food, as I spoon it on the dishes, and set it before them. As I sweep the floors, I hear its voice just beyond the raucous scrape of the broom. Ma-abu, it sings. It sings my name again. Ma-abu. I resist. But then it draws me away from the dark inner cave of the house, down to the stream's edge, coaxing me from all I am expected to do.

Giggling over stones, it rushes and wanders. I watch as nature herself quenches her thirst. All the birds and small beasts come to the edge of this water. They drink and are satisfied, and the birds bathe. Their quirky movements and teasing chattering make me smile.

They do not take it for granted, these beasts and birds. They cannot, they do not.

My tasks scold me, clamor for me. But they don't seem to know my name. Time and again the companion I have, this water, calls me back.

When I need it most, water, my friend, is there.

During the violence, then I cannot hear the water.

Only after, bleeding and broken, I crawl into the rain. As the cool water washes my cuts, I feel truly cleansed. I can bear anything.

With my throat dry and rasping from tears, I drink water slowly. It restores me, calms me.

I can bear all things.

Except one.

The heat and dry air, the diminishing stream, and I feel my world diminishing with it. The tears are frequent, the pain, too. The blood harder to remove as the water dries up. No clouds, no rain.

The water is somewhere, I know it. Its hiding place cannot be far, I tell myself.

And the terrible quiet.

It is the quiet that enlightens me. It is then I know. The birds and small beasts have gone to seek it. Hope blossoms in me, and I know as clearly as the water used to move over my feet what I must do.

I follow it, too.

Never before did I feel I could leave the pain, that I could walk away. But I do.

I pack two small biscuits and a bit of dried meat, my one extra chemise. I pack them in my shawl, and carry it and my shoes into the harsh daylight. I must leave now, while I can. I take comfort in knowing the light will fade soon and I will be gone before the sunlight's last rays touch the rooftop and die away into the night. Before they arrive back at this house, I will be indiscernible, in shadow.

I follow the dry streambed, dry but so visible in its simple weaving pattern. I go where the water has come from.

My heart is light.

When I find it, I will submerge myself in it. I will be made whole, as I never was before.

Passion  1

Never before had she felt this way, such raw power. M'cah could reach out her hand, she felt, and buildings would crumble, boats would capsize and shatter, doors would erupt into flame. Trees would crack and fall.

She trembled with the desire of knowing this power. It made her mouth water and then go dry.

Everything about her was stark and real. Objects took on a hard red outline, glowing as if in a bloody sunset or backed by a holocaust.

She doubted it not at all. It was there for her, at her fingertips. She coaxed it. Coursing through her, the power welled in a rush of heat through her center, taking hold of the marrow of her bones.

Never before, she thought, have I felt this way.

The power shone from her eyes.

Just look at me, M'cah thought, eyes seeking his. Just look and there will be no looking back, no escape from this black, red, unholy promise. This heat, this bloody surrender. Look at me, and you will be mine.

Look at me, and never again at her.

You will not see her again. Only me. You will not see her face. You will not feel her pain, only feel and see your own. You will not see your children's eyes, their sorrow, their pleading, or their joy.

All will be lost to you in this heat, in this moment. In me.

Look at me!

See nothing else. Blind. Foolish. Consumed. Flaming. Charred. Ruined. Broken. Blackened. Shattered. Dead. All dead.

Such power.

She lowered her hand, having just missed touching his.

The, his eyes met hers.

Floods of cold, water, quenching.

M'cah turned her face away. No spark, no fire.

No tragedies.

Slowly, she stepped away. Took another step, and then another. She walked away from him. He did not follow.

A tear slipped down her cheek. She poked at it with a finger, then slowly rubbed it into her palm. It cooled as it dried.

And she walked.

Passion  2

It's strange that it was days ago now—seven days to be exact—yet I find myself still pausing, ceasing to mend or clean or cook. I find myself still and silent. Not at all like myself.

And I think of what she said. And how she said it.

Even now. I busy my hands, beginning again to clean the turnips. I shake my head slowly, trying to erase the entire event, but I only succeed in scattering it around inside my head.

It congeals, draws itself back together and comes into focus.

She will never be able to return here, I tell myself, not for the first time. Never.

I shake my head again. And I realize that, again, my hands are still. I will never get the supper done at this rate. Keep your mind on your task, Aletha, I chastise myself.

I redouble my efforts, slamming the turnips into a kettle, pouring the water, and staring down into the movement of shadow and light in the water. Impatient with the turnips, with how slowly the water pours.

They rejected her. We all did. Now, every time anyone gathers together, all the talk is of her, how horrid she is, how wrong and crass and defiant. How did she dare to say such things? they all agree, shaking their heads, shaking their fingers, raising their shaking voices and fists, renouncing her words. Describing her using words that most of them would never normally utter.

And I have stayed silent. Or agreed, when pressed to do so.

And yet, what did she say that was not true?

I can't abide it. It troubles me so.

I remember well how she called out that one woman's name, and talked of how that woman had cheated her brother. She spoke of how the woman owned so much even before she stole from him, and how her brother felt such shame. They say he died of it. A man stood up and shouted, and drowned her out.

She spoke of my own cousin who was known to have forced himself on several of the women and who has never been held accountable for it. I know what he did. I know very well what he did. All these years I remained silent.

On that day, she stood up and spoke. On that day I could have died of shame.

I look down now, and see my own fingers digging into a turnip, ripping it apart though it hurts my fingers. Water has been splashed over the table. And I hear keening. I hear my own voice wailing.

And yet the shame was draining away. On that day I could have shouted my joy, my triumph. The truth. She saw it, knew it, spoke it.

The water is pink, my hands are still and the swells in the water are subsiding. Blood is oozing from two of my knuckles. I remove my hands from the water. And I throw the kettle to the floor.

After the noise dies away, I feel calm. I wrap my hand in a soft towel.

I am resolved.

I will find her. I will speak my truth. And I will be free.

The sun is shining as I leave the house. My neighbor calls to me. I ignore him. I believe I know where to find her; I have heard where she is.

I walk, straight and tall. I didn't even realize until now how bent I had felt, almost crouching through each day. And that had been coming on for years.

Not now. I am not free yet, not whole. But I will be. Aletha will speak, and Aletha will heal. And I will never come back here.

I smile.

Rebirth  1

She told me she loved me. Choza, I love you, she said. I didn't know what to say.

And she left. She asked nothing of me.

This is love? I thought. Hah.

Do you know? I never saw her again. After she said that. Yet she has been with me all this time. All these years. All these moments.

She came to me when I lay injured, in pain, waiting for, but not expecting help. I could not concentrate on her face. I wanted someone to be there who could eliminate the physical pain. Instead, she was there. But I do recall that, after she spoke to me, I slept.

Day after day, the pain lessened. And she was there. Even when she wasn't sitting right there next to me, I swear I could see her smile in the faces of those—some of those—who cared for me.

I saw her caring and compassion in some of the people who helped me as I recovered. Oh, it was a long, long road. It was grim. How I wanted to give up on feeling better. So many times I wanted to give up.

Then a helping hand would be extended to me. When I looked up at my helper, I expected to see her face. It was always another face, but with her smile. Or her eyes. The look of compassion.

And I walked again. In the beginning I believed I could not. But I did.

Now, I arise and walk, move about, almost without thinking of it. But, when I do recall, even when I feel a bit of pain, I feel so very grateful. Me, Choza, filled with gratitude.

She told me she loved me.

That is what I recall now, in addition to her compassion, her eyes, her smile.

Then, one day, I had such a surprise. It was a hot, steamy day. I had been working hard. I was looking into the stream, pulling up water in my cupped hand to splash on my face, to wash the sweat and grime away.

My hand paused on its way back to the surface of the water. The ripples slowly cleared.

I saw my face. Older than I remembered. Calmer than I remembered. I studied it and breathed deeply. I could feel the water drying and cooling on my face and hands. It was most pleasant.

I smiled.

It was her smile. The eyes, my eyes, held her compassion and understanding. I hadn't realized it was there.

I love you, I said out loud. Choza, I love you. I saw my lips move. And the smile remained.

A drop of water fell from my lifted hands. The water rippled and cleared again. I was not mistaken. There she was. Wearing my face, looking through my eyes, smiling my smile.

I ran my hand softly over the skin of the water, arose, and walked back to the wounded. I cared for them, held their hands, cooled their brows with wet cloths, whispered their names to them, and smiled at them.

My name is Choza, I said.

I told them that I loved them.

Rebirth  2

I don't talk so good. But I talk cuz you ask, get me?

No one like her. No one. We all here, all waiting. Don' know what for. Waiting, for food, for water, for nothing at all. We here cuz no there. See?

No there. No. No. Where go? Only here. Nowhere.

We all here. She come. She not like rest. No. Does not gotta be here. She got somewhere to go, see?

But, she here. See?

I no talk 'fore she come. Ruach keeps dumb. No. No. I keep dumb.

She talk me. Ask? No. Talk. And talk. Keep talk, all while here. Talk to all here.

She bring food, water. She talk. She feed. She talk. She give water. She talk.

Ask nothing.

Nighttime. All around fire try to keep, see? Keep warm. See? She bring covers, see? Um. See… blankets. That the word. She bring and give.

All sleep. Nighttime. Only me, Ruach, eyes wide. She see. She come. She sit. No talk. Not talk. We sit. And wait. Look into fire. Feed fire sometime. And sit.

I say, sleep. I say, see? To her. Not talk for long time. But I say, sleep.

She shake head. Not sleepy, she say, like that.

No, I say. Not sleepy.

We sit. Wait.

Why here? I say. She look. My eyes wide.

She smile at Ruach. Something like, where… see? She say, where else I be?

I no say, for a time. I say, not here.

No, she say. I need be here, she say.

We sit. She take out bread. Share. We eat.

I must sleep. Eyes closed. In darkness. Light when open eyes. She there, still wide eyes. She smile.

She stay, long time. Bring food, bring water, bring clothes. She talk. She hear.

I no talk, 'fore she come. I talk. See? Now. I see.

Soon. See? Soon. I talk more. I talk to them. She not here, I here. I talk. I hear. I see. I be here. Here. See?

Soon.

Mettle  1

My dear sister,

I do not know that this letter will ever get to you. I write it nevertheless, because I must.

The waiting is terrible. But it is almost over. I never knew one could welcome such an end. But that is how I feel.

Dawn is a short time away. There is no light in the sky, not yet. I can feel it, though, beyond the hills. Almost smell the sunrise.

I must write quickly.

Oh, dear one! I can scarce recall how we came to these straits. Yet it is so.

I harvested the grain. Do not be appalled, dear sister, at what I, Pey, your loving sister did. Do not judge me hastily.

I believe you knew we had been growing poorer each year, as so many have. Time and again, there were poor prices in the market, though our produce was so good.

You may not have heard. The season was upon us and we were prepared. My husband went to harvest one sunrise, and I did as I should, according to law. I shut up the house and washed and cleaned. No matter what you hear, be assured I did not show my face.

Night fell and he did not return. I prayed and I waited. I kept his supper ready and did not eat mine.

It was only as dawn broke that the neighbor arrived. He spoke loudly outside my door, as if to the walls and trees.

Pey, he called. He was silent for a time. Then he spoke of my husband's death. Yes, dear sister, from what I was able to gather, my husband collapsed in the fields.

He was buried. I did as expected. I stayed in the house and no one came near except when some man had to do so, to deliver goods. I stayed true to the law. I stayed unseen, and tried to mourn from inside my prison. Yes, that is what my house became to me. It was no longer a haven.

On the third evening I watched the sun sink through a small space in the blinds.

A fever came upon me. I'd never known anything like it. The fields, I knew, lay full of produce, all going to rot in the heat of the day, all unharvested. There was no man to harvest. No neighbor would do it. They had their own cares.

I made up my mind.

Each night for seven nights I went out in the black night and harvested. With my woman's hands, I harvested. I harvested the fruit of my husband's labors, for me and for my children.

Yes, sister, I broke the law.

I feel no shame. Sister, it is not an evil to share in the work. Oh, will you never know why I did it? No. You sha'nt. To even read my words would be counted on you as sin. I know it.

However, I feel no shame. I saved my children. They ate and were satisfied and no guilt falls to them. They are cared for.

I did what I needed to do.

Now, I finish these words, and I take them with me to the fire. You shall not see them, sister. Yet I pray that, somehow, you know.

Mettle  2

He was still talking. Suddenly Havah couldn't hear him. His voice was not there. His lips moved and his hands were animated. She stared with fascination at the pantomime. This silence shocked her. Nothing like this had ever happened before.

She found she could hear the children in the next room, but her husband's voice was gone. Strangely, she still knew everything he was saying, even without hearing his strident tones.

These rooms were not clean enough. Havah had spent hours dusting and sweeping, to no avail.

The supper she had made was inedible. She had walked to the market, which was quite a distance away for her. She had followed the instructions she'd been given for this dish. Havah was certain he would like it.

The children she was raising—their children—were hooligans. Toys were everywhere, though she had picked them all up not two hours ago. The two youngest were filthy, though she'd bathed them this afternoon. They were constantly loud, though she so often tried to entertain them, tell them stories, keep them quiet when he was home.

And she was too tired to please him.

Havah lowered her head when she realized that was the subject now. She could tell by the way he looked at her. She could tell by his gestures and sneer.

Too tired, he was saying, she was sure, though she still could not find his voice anywhere around her. Too tired to please him, even after quite obviously accomplishing nothing during this day.

She gazed at the floor, closed her eyes.

It was only when she dared look up that she knew his tirade was over, for the moment. He had left the room. She did not know which direction he'd headed.

She wandered, that night, from room to room. She wondered at her lack of tears, at how numb she felt all over. More than once Havah entered the children's room and stared at them as they slept. She studied them.

The pantomime began again at daybreak. He went on and on as she busied herself feeding and clothing the children. The silence was unsettling, but not truly unwelcome. She found solace in it, in a way. She gave each child a bit of food to take and saw them off to their teachers. She didn't even remember when her gesturing husband had left, when the pantomime had ended.

When all were gone from her house, she grabbed her broom and her cleaning cloths, and carried them up the street. She knocked on the door of an old, shabby house. The old man peered out, a smile appearing on his face. He hobbled back from the door, and spoke his loneliness. She entered, smiled, spoke, and made her offer. He was pleased.

Havah cleaned his two tiny rooms.

When she was done, they sat together for a few moments, sipping strong, hot tea. Then she said goodbye, gathered her supplies again, and carried them home.

She walked again to the market, and carefully made her selections. She hired a small boy to help her carry the goods. They walked together, side by side, to an old structure, and were welcomed. She and three women she had seen before but didn't know very well began to work together in the kitchen. They prepared the large meal and served it to the destitute men and women who resided there. There was much scraping of dishes clean, as these people ate and talked of gratitude for the meal. As Havah helped clean up, she laughed and spoke with the other helpers, and felt happy.

She left and went to retrieve her children from their lessons. When they arrived home, she fed them a simple meal and helped them each with the assignments they'd been given. Then they played games and she made up stories for them. They laughed with delight at her surprise endings, and she laughed in surprise with them. They laughed loudly, and were delighted.

He arrived home then. The house was filled with games strewn about, unwashed dishes, leftover food, and loud laughter. This time Havah heard his voice as he ordered the children out of the room and began to berate her. She could hear it now, though it came through softly, as if from another room, or through a warm blanket.

She sat and stared him in the eyes as he fumed, and he suddenly stopped. His anger was palpable. She felt like she could reach out and feel it, burning cold and burning hot, between them, if she had wanted to do so. She did not reach out.

Calmly, Havah rose. She announced, I cleaned the old man's house today. I helped cook and serve a large meal for the destitute today. I helped the children with their lessons and played with them today.

As for pleasing you, I know I never have and I never can.

He was silent.

Havah strode into the next room, and began to play with her children.

Consolation  1

I can remember vividly the moment the physician told me the news, told me of the illness.

I can remember the feel of the cloth of my skirt against my thigh, and the heat from the palm of my hand. My fingers smoothed the skirt free of wrinkles. I heard a voice rise in laughter somewhere down in another room. The sunlight slanted through the small window, playing with the leaf shadows on the wall.

The physician's voice was low. Then he stopped speaking. I remember a hand coming to rest on my shoulder, my husband's hand. Morea, he said softly. I did not respond.

I can remember all that, all those details.

But I can't remember how I felt.

These days, I can remember how much or how little I manage to accomplish each day. I can count the hours when I could not concentrate on anything. I can recall the number of times my body was wracked with pain.

But I can't remember really feeling anything.

There was a time when I remembered nothing; the illness took time and memory from me. I was empty. I do remember when they told me I had been away—unconscious—for days, weeks. How my husband thought he'd lost me. Morea, he cried. I did not respond.

Strangely, as I walked through the streets this morning at dawn, I felt something for the first time since that day when the physician's news took my emotions from me. It wasn't fear that I felt. I thought most certainly it would be that or anger. Depression.

No. I was relieved. I stood, watching the sky get lighter. And I felt relief.

Slowly, I made my way back to the house and sat down by the window. My husband came through, on his way out to work. He stopped a moment and asked, Morea, are you all right?

Could I tell him how relieved I felt? Could I possibly express the sheer joy of feeling that, of feeling something, and of all things, relief?

I only smiled at him and said I was fine. He paused a moment longer, kissed me rather awkwardly, then was gone.

I didn't exactly feel energetic. But the relief stayed with me, helped me decide what to do. And I accomplished a number of things.

For the first time in months I had a meal ready, waiting for my husband when he came in. He was surprised. I helped him take off his coat. I sat and listened as he expressed frustrations about his work and then told me about the people he'd encountered during the day.

Our conversation was easy. He told a joke and we both laughed. We lingered over our wine.

We made love that night. He was tender and patient. I was pleased I could make him happy.

Later, I watched him as he slept. And again, that marvelous sense of relief washed over me. It had been with me all day, and now it poured out of me. I had the sense that he felt it, too, that it had made our lovemaking tender and special. That he felt it even now, as he was sleeping peacefully.

I wanted to tell him all that I understood.

I could not.

How could I explain that, while I may be dying, I also know that I am living?

Consolation  2

They are not invited. But they will come anyway.

I patched my only dress as best I could, put on my shawl to hide the stains. I combed my hair again and again. I washed my face and left it plain.

Slowly I prepared… not for them. Not for any of them. For me. I did this for me.

Again and again, I checked my small bag. The coins were there. The silver glinted even in the darkness of the cloth bag. I was mesmerized for a time, then closed the bag again.

The small necklace had brought more coins to me than I had thought it would. My sole remaining possession—no longer mine. It had not been as difficult to let it go as I had thought it would be.

They began to arrive, just as I thought they would. Gossiping and pretending to comfort. Shiha's only son, I heard them whisper. The audacity of saying to each other, and Shiha doesn't appear to mourn.

Under my shawl, I fingered the cloth bag with the coins inside. It soothed me.

To lose her husband, and now this…

The cloth, the feeling of round coins, they comforted me.

Her eyes are dry…

Has Shiha even cried?

I have no tears left, I could have told them.

What I heard…

They mingled, spoke words to me that I did not hear, and that I do not care to hear. I could hear their gossiping and whispering to each other, but I did not know what they said directly to me.

They tried to get me to eat. I felt no more hunger and refused their offerings.

And, all at once, it seemed that all sound in the room faded. The people still moved, their limbs, their lips, but I heard nothing, except the calling, whispering of a voice I know so well.

From the dark doorway of the room, he stepped. He looked at me. Mother, was all he said.

Lifted by his presence, I rose slowly and walked toward him—calm, at peace. I took his arm. Together we walked toward the door. No one impeded us. If anyone spoke to me, I did not hear.

His arm was real, solid, the muscle hard under the warm skin.

Do they call my name? Shiha, Shiha…

Together, side by side, we walked out the door into the cool evening, the dusk still hanging in the sky to the east, purplish and hazy, and fading gold to the west.

I stared at the pinkish clouds as they lost their blush.

We walked, silent for a time. I was filled with a great, deep happiness and a heavy sadness, all at once. It made my knees quiver, these myriad, conflicting feelings.

I slowed as we neared the grassy slope with its one small tree. The full moon slid up behind us just as the sun's last glow died on the opposite horizon.

He tried to continue, right up to the top of the small hill, but I stopped, unable to proceed, pulling at his arm.

Mother, he said again.

Yes, I said. Yes, I say to myself, I am your mother, yes, I am. Yes, I mourn your father. Yes, I am alone. Yes, I say again, out loud.

His warm arm slipped from mine. The rising breeze chilled me. Blisteringly cold where his arm left mine. I shivered.

Yes, my son.

He moved away, so far away I could not reach him from where I stood.

Good night, my son. It is only right, I tell him and myself.

It is here they find me.

The crowd is with me again. Slowly we move away from my son's grassy resting place.

The crowd is whispering still, as they steer me away. I hear them whisper my name. Shiha, Shiha…

They do not see that he is still with me, his warm, strong arm holding my own.

Long after the crowd thins and leaves, we sit, my son and I, together in the dark house. As the sun rises, we join hands and begin our long walk, leaving the grassy slope behind. We leave it all, all the sorrow, behind.

I finger the coins again. We will be fine. He is always with me.

Keeper  1

I supported my father. For years, long years before others my age worked long hard hours, I worked. An important servant in an important household—that was my father.

I cooked and cleaned for him.

I cooked and cleaned for our master and mistress, when told to do so.

I pulled water and carried it, walked to the market and haggled over goods and food, all before I'd seen 14 summers.

And, when my father said, Agdie, lie down, I did. When he did it, I lay back on the mat, closed my eyes, and waited for him to be done.

The places I went to in that time only I know about. And I don't share those.

I supported my brother. For years, long years I waited upon him, cleaned his messes, kept him from our father's wrath, took the punishment in his place, found him coins when he demanded. An unimportant being in an important household—that was my brother.

I cared for him.

I loved him.

I protected him.

Agdie, I go.

And, when he left, I mourned him, even as I cooked and cleaned and submitted.

I supported the man my father chose for me. For years, long years I slaved for him. An unimportant man longing to be an important one, to be acknowledged, to be elevated, to be great—that was my husband.

I cooked for him.

And I cleaned for him.

I pulled water and I carried it. I walked to the market and haggled over goods and food.

And, when he said, Agdie, lie down, I did. And when he did it, I lay back on the mat, closed my eyes, and was glad when he was done, and was glad it was no longer my father who ravaged me.

I conceived and bore three children. On my own, I cared for them as I cared for him. My only joys, they died all of them, before I had seen 28 summers.

And when my husband died, I, a widow, bore the grief of untold work, of heavy years, of loss, of an unacknowledged, unwanted life. An invisible life.

Unencumbered by father, brother, husband, even children, I, Agdie, came upon salvation.

I support my savior. For many years now, I have done so. The most important person in my world, that is my savior.

I cook for her.

I clean for her.

I pull water and carry it. I market. I sing. For the first time, I sing. I speak. I have a voice.

She listens to me, to Agdie. There is nothing in all existence that is like being heard. Being seen. Being listened to.

And when she bids it, I listen to her.

We are not mistress and slave, but women, working together. I did not know this world existed. Since coming to it, I know great peace, a serenity that was only distantly dreamed of and sobbed over in great agony. Here, it is real. I live it, each day.

The places I go now, I sing about.

I know what it is to laugh, to nurture, to work, and to play.

I am acknowledged.

I am.

Keeper  2

When it comes over me, I am not myself. I am there, but standing to one side, unable to move, looking on in horror. I cannot tell the time that passes when it is upon me.

When it is done, I am so very tired.

Still, they inquire of me, time and again, Zab, what is wrong? What is wrong with you?

I can be well for a time—almost believing life can be as I remember it once was. Then they ask again, sometimes with fear, sometimes with loathing, why? Why do you do that? Why do you behave that way?

I no longer try to explain how I am not doing anything… that I simply have to wait for it to be done before I can be myself again.

It first came upon me when I was young and happened not very often. As I grew into the beginnings of womanhood, it became more frequent.

It was then the inquiries became intense and fearful. Zab, Zab, why are you this way? What comes over you? It was then they told me I said strange things, even appeared to predict strange occurrences. It mattered not at all that these claims I made did not come true.

They pestered me. My mother, my sisters and brothers. Always wanting to know why, why.

When I came out of one of these, I was resting as I always needed to. When I opened my eyes, I saw my mother sitting beside me. I knew she was there to speak of it, but I only wanted to sleep. Still, she began. Zab, she sighed. She told me that no man would want me if this continued, that my family would not be able to protect me.

I was so very tired, but I became even more frightened. I could feel my heart beating faster and faster, almost like I was in the grip of a spell.

I don't remember her leaving my bedside.

I stayed awake, frightened, all night.

I stayed frightened, for months.

Then came the day of my liberation. We had all, as a family, walked to the market. I felt rather tired from no sleep, but all seemed to be well otherwise.

Then, I heard the whisperings, of neighbors and strangers. Zab, I heard. Amongst their words, I heard my name.

My heart began to beat furiously again. No, not now, I pleaded to my tormentors.

Then I was down, and once again, standing to the side. I watched as my own family pulled back from me, faces full of fear, hatred, and disgust.

A tall woman walked through the crowd that had gathered around and yet had drawn away from my prone body, writhing in the dust. She strode calmly through the crowd, directly up to me, and knelt beside me.

Her slim hand reached out toward my head, and even standing where I was, observing, I felt cool fingers on my brow. I closed my eyes and listened to a comforting voice. I could not hear the words, but I knew they were words of love and acceptance.

When I opened my eyes, I had returned to myself. She was there, the tall woman, still kneeling beside me. Concern on her face, but a smile too. The crowd was still there, still hanging back, falling into silence.

My name is Zab, I said clearly.

She helped me up and gazed into my face. She started to ask me a question and I flinched, expecting the usual Why.

Instead I heard, Zab, how do you feel?

I followed her to her home and she welcomed me.

When I see those who were my family, I smile, say polite things and then I go home.

And on the rare occasions when the fit comes upon me, she is there to lay a cool hand on my brow and cheek, to talk to me until I return, and I always do.

I am not so very afraid anymore.

Sustenance 1

Each day is the same. I reach for food canisters, measure out what my family needs to sustain us this day.

And I pray.

Then I dole it out, with whispered thanks for our needs being met this day, for my children, my husband, his mother and sister.

Nakavoa, they say, thank you.

And we proceed through the day, doing our separate and communal tasks for this family—as our children take their lessons from me, and their aunt and grandmother sew and help with the house chores, and their father, my husband, goes out again to find work for the day—sometimes finding it, sometimes not.

We find in each day something quite wonderful—the children will find a stone with a purplish hue, the aunt brings home a funny story or two about the neighbor's chickens, the grandmother sings an old song, and teaches us the words and tune. Even my husband smiles at the memories his sister and mother tell.

In the evening when we sit down together at our table, to share what we have, I tell of two more souls who wandered by, haunted eyes telling of poverty, displacement, fading hope.

No one asks, but they know that I again reached for the food canisters to place some small offering in the hand of each person, with a blessing to spare, as they went on their way. I grow silent, the story told.

I can feel the silent prayers around me, lifted up almost in unison, almost sounding in my ears like one of grandmother's songs. My prayer rises with theirs.

Nakavoa, I can almost hear them say, we understand. We all do.

As the sun sets, we play with the children, then put them to bed. Then we turn to rest, or we sit together, speaking quietly about the children, and not about the haunted souls.

And we sleep.

And at dawn, the day begins as the last one did. I reach for the canisters, and prepare food for my family.

And I pray. With whispered thanks for our needs being met this day, I turn to my tasks for the day.

It is enough.

Sustenance  2

Hoam was having trouble making up her mind that it was the right thing to do. At times, she was convinced about the path she was about to take, at others she was quite uncertain.

There was really no one to ask. There was her father, but he was often absent, even when right beside her. And his view, well, it was always the easiest-looking path that attracted him.

And her friends, it appears to her that they made their choices the same way.

Everyone said, Hoam, he is a fine, upstanding man, destined to be a leader in the community. There was no doubt he could support her, and her father as well, if need be.

It seemed the thing to do, at times, to bind her life to his.

Yet, it was his expectation that she could not do otherwise that made her hesitate, and anger flared at times. And her father's expectation, too, made her wince with hurt and rage. And he would try to frighten her into it, too, if he perceived for one moment that she was resisting the possibility.

The easy path.

It was what Hoam's mother had done, her father told her, and his mother, too.

Hoam had no means of knowing that. They had long since died. How she longed to speak with them, ask them her many, many questions. Especially this question.

What should I do?

Or, perhaps she'd ask, should I do what is expected of me?

And there were no other prospects, her father continually reminded her. And she was getting older.

At this Hoam couldn't help but smile secretly. She was young still.

She shook her head, trying to get the troubling thoughts to fall into some kind of order or fall out of her head. She closed her eyes again, tried to fall asleep.

Her eyes opened of their own accord and she sighed as she pushed back the blanket and stood up.

The moon was full, and she walked out into the bluish light, into a warm, scented breeze. She sat down, her back against the stone wall, which seemed both cool and warm, as if it held the sense of both night and day.

Closing her eyes, she breathed deeply, trying to sort out which flower scent she could detect on the breeze. Lilac, she thought, and it made her happy. And sad. It was the scent of her mother. For years after her death, some of her clothing held that scent. She had managed to take a few of her mother's things without her father noticing. He would not have approved. It was as if he thought of her mother as being only in the past. Maybe she was for him.

Dimly, Hoam felt she could see her mother again, like a figure painted in moonlight hues. She had experienced this before and it filled her with a sense of tranquility. Those racing thoughts slowed, stopped, departed.

Yet something was different this time. She waited patiently, pushing away the unknown excitement, as the second figure materialized. Both figures wavered as if stirred in the air, then the light of the beings, shining from within, grew more solid and with dimension.

She felt awe as they approached her. A calm expectancy. Anticipation.

It was her mother. She knew it, even though she often felt she'd forgotten her mother's features. It has been so long, she thought. But it was her mother.

And her grandmother—a woman she had never met. Her mother's mother.

Hoam knew such joy. And the awe returned as these two bright beings held out their arms, smiled serenely at her, and began to sing to her.

The music rooted her and uplifted her. This song, without real words, was filled with meaning—a love for her that she hadn't felt since... well, for many years.

The music, the love, their smiles enveloped her. Without even knowing she moved, she stood and lifted her arms with theirs, and began to sing. She felt a brightness in herself, a vivid glow that matched and met theirs, until their bodies were one light, their voices one song.

All too soon, it seemed to her, those glowing arms embraced and released, the song faded, and she stood alone in the night, the full moon off to her left where it had been on her right.

She had tears of joy on her face, splashed on her tunic.

If she told anyone, they would tell her she was dreaming. Or think she was crazy.

The first ray of sunlight beamed on the horizon, splashing the edges of her gaze, warming her right cheek and brow, as she continued to stand on the warm, cool stone. She turned to face it. Hoam would tell no one. It was no dream, and she would keep it to herself.

Later that morning she made tea and cakes and served them to her father and the man who was so certain of her. And she told him she would not marry him.

The moonlight, the hues, the song filled her heart, and she was at peace in the storm that followed.

Lessons  1

Sumana, who is brave? he asked me. No one, he said, bitter and angry.

I said nothing, at first.

Courage, there is no such thing.

I knew he was angry with himself and yet raising his voice to me. I took a deep breath and raised my eyes to his face.

He sensed my defiance before I said a word.

No, no, he said, courage…

My mother was brave, I said softly, but firmly. He stared at me. I smiled inside, to myself. She was the most courageous person I have ever known, I said solemnly.

And I said no more, to him. He had waited a moment, waited for me to justify my statement, explain how a woman could be brave. Then he stormed out of the room, and out of the house.

Now I really smiled so that anyone could see, if anyone had been there.

It was years ago, several years before I married and left my mother's house. I was young and quite vain. The girls I spent time with talked only of vain things—their hair, their beauty, catching a boy's eye. It was all that mattered.

I thought it had been all that mattered to me, too.

There came a day when I ran into an acquaintance when my mother and I went to buy food for our evening meal. We talked and laughed, waiting to see if any boys our age would make an appearance near the market place, while our mothers or their maids shopped the stalls.

It was then she appeared. I immediately felt loathing, and shame as well. I turned my eyes away from her, but not before I caught her defiant gaze.

And the gossiping began. All around me the voices buzzed, the voices of my friends; then, like wildfire, catching the faces and voices of mothers, maids, and some of the men.

I tried to say nothing, to be invisible. And then I laughed that derisive laugh with them. And, I feel shame over that to this very day.

Without my realizing it, my mother had come up and was standing behind me. She heard the hateful thing that was uttered and witnessed my joining in, ridiculing that girl, the defiant, raggedy girl.

My mother's face was stone as she grasped my upper arm. Without saying a word to me or the other mothers, participants, and onlookers, she walked me over to the ridiculed one.

I had tried to dig in my heels, to protest loudly. I could not.

My mother spoke to her, spoke in kind words with a soft, benevolent voice—the exact opposite of the iron grip she had on me. I didn't catch what she said, for my face felt like it was burning off and my ears felt full of cotton.

I tried to glance up and saw the strangest look on the girl's face, but I turned from it.

After what seemed a long time, my mother released her hold and we walked, alone, toward home. She was silent much of the way. Then she began to speak. Sumana, she said, in a calm, firm voice. She told me the defiant girl's story, of once being rich, but also being the daughter of a man accused and convicted of crimes, of stealing and fraud. Then he ran away with the little of their family goods that were left, and was never seen again.

The mother had found little jobs to do, but never was able to make a good home for herself or her daughter. There were rumors that she took in men and pleased them, for money.

None of this had been in the words of all of those marketplace gossipers. None of the truths my mother spoke were there in those tattling tongues and vicious stories.

She, my mother said finally, opening our door and turning to me, she never did anything wrong. Sumana, you tell me. Should she be so punished?

Then my mother turned and went into the house.

I stood for a long time on our doorstep and then slowly I went inside. I had remembered, while I stood there, that some of my mother's words to that young woman included an invitation to dine with us. I felt shame and dread, and really disliked my mother—and myself—at that moment.

The dreaded time arrived, and the meal was shared. I was sitting across from our raggedy guest. And I realized that the look she'd given me, as my mother was speaking to her so publicly, was a look of pity.

Once again, my face felt like it was on fire. She, pitying me.

Then I saw why. She felt sorry for me because of the public speaking, and knew how she'd have felt if the places, our places, had been reversed.

I felt such surprise at that moment. I looked up. Her eyes were upon me. I smiled at her.

It was the first time I'd ever felt even slightly brave myself.

She smiled back.

And I smile again today. That girl often came to our house. And we became the object of gossip and even became somewhat ostracized for a time. But it passed, and she, she and I, grew up under the firm, compassionate, brave eyes of my mother.

Yes, I said out loud, the bravest souls I ever knew, the both of them.

Urtha:

You have traveled far; you must be weary.
Come into my home.
I am preparing for you, for all your needs.
Let me serve you; it is my greatest desire.
Rest, and take your ease.
This is your home, your family,

Ramy:

You have much to teach; I need to learn.
Come into my heart.
You are prepared for me; you know my needs.
Let me hear you; it is my greatest desire.
Speak, and I will listen.
You are my home, my family.

Urtha and Ramy:

Teach us
when to prepare and when to welcome,
when to act and when to be still.
Resurrect for us
faith when we doubt,
hope when we mourn.
Reveal to us

that which is better,
that which is lasting.
May we prepare for your arrival.
May we run out to meet you.
And welcome your presence.
And sit at your feet.
And listen.
May we open our homes to you.
May we open our hearts to you.

Emergence  1

I stood on my own, as my father taught me. Independent, as it was beaten into me. I stood alone, always alone.

I needed no one. That was weakness, in my eyes, and anyone who was at all intelligent about such things knew that. It was the only type of person I could respect, that I wanted to know. Dependence is weakness. Asking for anything was unheard of in my world.

So the women, who could understand them? I couldn't. I got tired of listening to the semi-constant descriptions of feelings, of asking me, Lowano, what I was feeling. Anger, mostly, I'd end up saying. That engendered a number of responses, including, oh, let me help you or reactive anger. I preferred the latter. I didn't need help, you see.

I'd change the subject. I'd ask what she thought of our leaders, of the punishment doled out to a certain criminal, of the role of women and/or the rules against women in sacred issues. Invariably, this ended in tears, recriminations, anger, silence, or a mixture of these.

It made me feel strong, switching the conversation from feelings and evoking them from my target instead. I was so powerful. I truly enjoyed it. Power and arguments on my terms. I enjoyed each tear, because it fed my power and proved I was right—I was convinced of it. And I was convinced I'd beat her down with my words, with my powerful words—my power to persuade. I'd change her mind. Yes, I, Lowano, would be able to change her mind. If not now, eventually.

Ultimately, I was convinced, I would be able to mold her into what she ought to be. It became my sacred duty.

And then she would leave. I was always stunned, hurt, angry. There were those emotions again. Evoking, again.

I would try again after a time, trying this time to see her potential for leaving early on when we first met, so I could work my way around it, and have her so involved in the conversations—in the individual conversations as well as the longer, ongoing one—that she didn't feel able to leave. Emotionally involved. Turn them on her.

It always worked. For a time. And then it wouldn't.

The last time—I'm not sure I can tell the story. Yet, I must. I've been told that it will help me. Me. Lowano. Who did not need help.

She walked away from me—walked away from all the individual conversations, one by one. And then she walked away from the entire conversation.

I kept trying. Persuading. Convinced of my persuasiveness. She wasn't going to get away. I pestered her. I... bullied her with words. Or, I tried to... she was not listening anymore.

Those emotions. Again. I had never felt such rage. She wasn't listening to me. And then she wasn't listening at all. Not to anyone.

Even when she moved no more, spoke no more, breathed no more, the rage continued, accompanied by strong, strange elation. Then the emotions subsided, throughout the incarceration, the questioning, the trial, the pronouncements, to this moment.

When I finally realized she was gone, I was overcome by emotions—not all of which I could name. It wasn't that she just wasn't responding—she couldn't. She ceased.

For the first time, I asked for help. The emotions controlled me, and I asked for help.

Another woman. She came and she talked to me and she listened. It was she who said I must speak out what I have done.

She's helped me see something that I couldn't before—that she, the one who died, didn't respect the power I felt when I bullied her. Bully is her word, by the way, not mine.

Still, how did I miss that, I wonder? Why didn't I know that?

I see, now, that I might have asked for help sooner. I feel weak now, but not because I asked for help. Because I didn't do it sooner.

Of course, none of this will save me. My time will come, sooner, much sooner than I would like.

It's strange. Strange to realize it only now. There is great strength in her refusal to be a part of that conversation.

There is great strength in seeking help and being able, then, to accept. That has taken me the rest of my life to learn.

There is great strength in not always sermonizing, but in listening. In listening.

There is great power there. Even I could not still that power. She is powerful still. The power I sought, she already had.

Emergence  2

The time, my father said, is against women. And girls.

His face was so sad and tired, but his voice was patient and there was a surprising intensity to it. Yet he spoke so quietly.

You never knew, after all, who might be listening. As he had said, often enough.

My mother sat very still. Her gaze fixed on the floor. I was mortified as one large, translucent tear edged out of her right eye and sped down her face, to hang, hesitantly, off her chin. And then dropped. The trail it left was so small, I thought absurdly. She appeared to not have noticed.

This was her sister, I told myself silently, and the reality of it scorched me inside, like a sharp, hot knife slicing. Her sister. Always, she'd been my Aunt, but the close relationship, sister to sister, had never truly occurred to me before this moment.

And now it had, because Aunt was gone.

I glanced back at my mother, the sister with no sister anymore. Her face was now dry, her mouth set.

Elbet, my father murmured to me, and was quiet. Then he said, she spoke out... against the hypocrisy. The… misinterpretation of our sacred writings. My father's voice was little above a whisper.

Yes, my mother agreed.

Aunt. Sister. Sister-in-law.

She'd been a friend to me, as well. A confidant. How could there be a world without her?

My father looked at me, surprise showing in his eyes. I was surprised, too. I hadn't realized I'd asked this question out loud. But he nodded.

It was my mother who spoke.

Yes, Elbet, she said, I wonder that too.

I stood, tentatively, like someone standing up in a boat, afraid to rock it too hard. I swayed a little as I moved slowly to sit down beside my mother.

Your sister, I said, still plumbing the depths of that sorrow.

My mother grasped my shoulders, and then embraced me. Her arms strong, her body warm. We cried softly, trying to keep the whole-hearted sobs at bay.

When the wave of sorrow subsided, and the tears with it, my father said, You must admire her, Elbet, my daughter. Things will be said about her. Terrible things. Lies. It has already begun. But you must admire what she did… in private. Quietly, with us. Else others in our family will be ruined. Even killed.

I knew what he was saying, but the injustice of it made me want to snap at him. I looked at my mother. Once again, she gazed at the floor. She said nothing. She did not move. Her eyes were dry.

The family. Already so many lost, for reasons no one could truly comprehend – this imagined slight against a powerful religious leader, that misinterpreted phrase, this suspicion due to relationship. So many were simply not seen again.

No one so close to us really, until now. Aunt. Sister. Sister-in-law. Friend.

We will walk quietly in this time, my father assured us, and himself. We will remember her, here, among us. And what she did.

He looked at me. There was a desperation in his voice as he said, Do you understand, daughter? His anxiety was palpable. I could have reached out and touched its cold, prickly surface, resting invisibly between us. And yet the warmth of love was there, too.

I could not find my voice, so I nodded. And I said to him, in my mind… do you understand, father, that I will follow in her footsteps? Take up her cause? That I must? When my time comes?

My mother nodded.

Insight 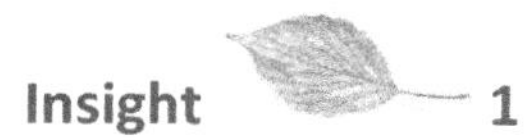 1

Oh, grandmother Kela, she cried as she sailed into the room and fell at my feet, grasping my two hands in her own.

My child, I said, what is it?

I knew the core problem—one of young love and a breaking, young heart. I felt her pain, it came off her in waves, almost visible in the fading light.

Child, I repeated, as she gathered herself and attempted to stop sobbing. Cry, N'asa, I said to her, for trying to stop it will make it all the harder on you.

She let the tears fall, her face in my lap, my hands on her head, fingers gently combing through the soft strands of hair.

The tempest ceased quite suddenly. Still, she was silent for a time, waiting until she could breathe deeply again without catches and sobs.

Oh, grandmother. The voice was soft and sad.

Tell me.

Mother has denied him. Refused.

Now there was anger in her voice.

She has said that we may not marry!

I continued to stroke her hair, waiting, in case there was more.

Grandmother Kela! You must help!

N'asa, what do you mean?

Her eyes were bright and full of hope as she finally met my gaze. The ideas were just coming to her, that she could come to me for comfort, but perhaps also for help.

Tell me what your mother said to you, I sighed.

She denied him!

Yes. But what did she say?

She… she listens to rumors! She told me he is a bad man. A hypocrite. Greedy. Gossip, that's all it is. Will you help us?

Child, I said again. I again took both her hands in mine and I contemplated, studying her beautiful face, tear-streaked though it was. Inside myself, I asked the Spirit to give me the words to speak.

I told her, gently, that I wanted only her happiness. And that her mother wanted that as well. She scoffed, but I raised my hand, and asked her to listen.

I told her that rushing into anything is what foolish people do.

I told her that when an old woman sits in the market place, she hears and sees many things.

Her eyes were bright still, but not with tears. N'asa was calculating where my words were going. But she was listening.

I sighed. I, too, have heard the rumors and the gossip. You know me, child. Do I give credence to the things I hear?

No, grandmother. You give credence to… what you know.

To what I have experienced. Now, I will tell you a little something, if you will hear it.

Yes.

Long ago, before I met your grandfather, I loved a man.

No! Kela… Her eyes were bright, this time with wonder and a bit of mischief.

Yes. Listen now. I fancied I had found the man for me. My father, your great-grandfather, refused him. I was horrified, hurt, and felt as if hope and my heart had been ripped from me. By my own father. Oh, I was so angry.

Her hand fluttered to rest on her breast. She sighed. She knew the feeling.

I told her, I rarely felt anger toward my father. I couldn't remember a time, until that moment. I was ready to flee, to find that man and run off with him.

Her lips parted. I heard the intake of breath and then, Oh.

Yes, very unlike me. I smiled. Wouldn't you say?

She nodded, saying nothing.

Yes. Very unlike me. I had no mother to turn to… she died two years before. I convinced myself that she would have seen the situation as I did. Then… my aunt, my mother's sister, came to me. I found out much later that my father sought her help in this situation. You see, he hated denying me anything. But he knew what I did not.

I smiled. Pushed a strand of hair out of my granddaughter's face.

Child… she did not try to convince me one way or the other.

What did she say? The voice was a whisper, wanting to know and not wanting to know.

She said, Kela, we can only know a person by her actions. Or, in this case, his actions. What he says matters, true. But what he does matters more.

I let the silence draw out. My granddaughter looked away from me for a time, toward the last of the fading light as it changed the colors of the walls in the room. Her eyes remained fixed there for a time. When she looked back at me, the dusk had filled the room, but I could see her eyes clearly.

What did you do, grandmother? She asked. Her voice was soft, but steady. There was still sadness in her voice, yet strength as well. And no tears.

I sought the truth.

A moment passed, and she nodded.

Did I help you, dear one? I asked. I wanted to say more, even to plead with her. But I did not.

Thank you, grandmother.

She rose, still meeting my gaze. Then she kissed me on the forehead, just as her mother had often done. The similarity in them, at that moment, touched and reassured me.

It's getting dark in here. Let's join mother in the other room.

Yes, child of my child.

Insight  2

He spoke words that conjured such images in my mind. But images they were, not real. Tales to be told and not necessarily believed.

You will have fine clothes, such garments as you've never seen, Mareppa. Gold and silver fabrics. Royal blue and purple. Fit for a queen.

At what price? I asked myself in silence.

Jewelry! He said as if he'd just thought of it. Such gold and silver there, on your white neck, your arms, your ankles.

Chains, I thought.

Such abundant food, he boasted. Parties. Tasty tidbits from far away, exotic lands. Delicacies to delight you, Mareppa. Only you.

Poison, to me.

A place. Position of honor. Of stature in our community.

Burdens to bear.

Money. All you want or need, to buy all that you desire, he purred.

Debts to owe you.

A fine palace. I'll build it for you, with all that you want in it. Many rooms, all to be decorated to your taste.

A prison.

All this I give to you, Mareppa, he said. He looked at me smugly, expectantly—even greedily, wanting a surfeit of gratitude and a cringing display of my unworthiness at his show of generosity and wealth.

So. Speaking out loud this time. At what price?

His smile lost a bit of its feigned warmth.

What was that?

This was not what he expected. Clearly.

I asked you. At what price?

You have but to agree.

To what?

To be my mistress. Smugly again, but with a sharp light coming to his eyes.

I smiled. He smiled, appearing to find my smile to his liking.

No.

His smile waned and was gone. Mareppa. I will bring you out of poverty! His voice was edged with anger. I hated the way his oily voice oozed and then spat my name.

I am not poor.

He stared, his cheeks and neck growing red.

Not poor! He hissed the words.

I looked out the window, over the meadow, following the soaring birds and noting the gold of the waving grain. I gazed around my little cottage, quietly measuring in my mind the cloth I have for clothes and the food in my pantry. And the few coins I have, resting solidly in my pocket. And the garden of food growing outside my door, nearly ready for harvest.

I picked up my needle again, and continued to mend my cloak.

You would have security! He sputtered.

I am secure, I say. I am not concerned. I have much for which to be grateful.

I smile at him.

He cannot think of anything else to say. With a last grunt of anger and disapproval, he heaved his heavy body out of the chair, grunting fouls words, and left my home.

I am free.

Subversive  1

I fought her at first. I fought against what she said, what she did.

Such arrogance, I thought. Unbecoming in a woman. So ill conceived. I refused to see the good she did. I could not believe anything I heard about the help she provided. She's up to something, I told others.

It became a vocation. Where others extolled her virtues, I spoke of her immaturity and insolence, shouting others down when I had to.

Words never came to me so easily. I believed with a fervor I'd never before experienced, fueled by hate and a blind ignorance. I clung to my beliefs, spoke loudly at every chance that presented itself.

Still, she moved on slowly among the people in our community, touching them, speaking to them, listening, caring, healing.

I raged. Waves of epistles issued from me with an eloquence I did not think I had within me. I loved those words. I relished in forming them, noting the workings of my tongue and lips. Speaking them, spitting them. Raging, belittling, refuting, roaring.

She continued, doing as she'd done.

Do not trust her! I screamed.

Galbra is right, they said in response. Eventually, they agreed with me.

Her hands reached out, weaving a fabric of love and acceptance, so filmy I could not see it, yet so strong.

Then, I stood, one day, on my usual spot, describing in detail the sin of her ways, the arrogance, the…

A sharp sensation took my breath. I realized I was alone. How long, I wondered, had I been alone? Others were here, I told myself, but a moment ago. They raised their voices, too. In tirades, accusations. Their voices raised with mine. Never as loud as mine, but there.

Words failed me. People passing by turned tentatively toward me, wondering at my silence. They did not stop. They hurried on, refusing to look into my eyes.

I could feel my face grow hot. They were embarrassed for me. For me, Galbra.

A woman paused, a woman who had raised her voice with mine. When had she gone from me, from my side? I wondered. I did not know. How long had I been alone? I spoke to her softly, but she moved on, pretending she hadn't heard me call her name.

After a moment, I turned toward my home, walking slowly, trying to work up the hatred, the fervor that had been so long my companion.

My sister stood defiantly at the front door as I approached, slowly giving way to me to let me in. She led toward the front room. What is it? I asked brusquely. I wanted to think, not to hear whatever petty concerns she had. I could see something on her face and wanted the conversation to be brief.

Your littlest one, Galbra. She's been ill. Her voice was steady and reedy with emotion barely contained.

All thoughts fled as I pushed passed her to the inner room, and knelt next to my child's bed. My child smiled up at me, a tired by heartfelt smile.

Oh, my child, I cried, and the hot tears burned my face.

Then my sister gently pulled me away. She steered me back to the other room, sat me down. In moments she put tea in front of me. Then she sat down and spoke softly. She told me of taking my child to that woman for healing.

Concern turned to rage. I began to stand, readying my lungs for a scream, for words of indictment and accusation. That woman!...

Your child lives, Galbra, she whispered, because of that woman. The words were soft, but I heard them.

My sister stood slowly when she saw the words and rage drop out of me without being given voice. Think on that, she said.

In a few days, my child was able to be with me as I took my short journey in steps, but a long journey in so many other ways. I stepped softly on my hatred and ignorance, my sharp words sending pain shooting into me at each step. But tread I did, carrying my child to the woman's house.

She came to the door, smiling at me in a way that made me feel even greater shame, even sharper pain.

I thank you, I stuttered. For my child's life.

She placed her hand on my arm. She said nothing to me at first, but asked my child how she was feeling. I listened to my daughter, content to do so.

One more time I spoke. I took my old position in public and I praised her and thanked her and apologized to her and to all. The words came haltingly at first, and then I relished, savored them—ever so much more than the other words.

Subversive  2

My mother knew. Let me tell you of her last story with him.

She worked hard, very hard. Her whole life was work. She fed us and kept us warm, told us stories, comforted us.

We were not her own, not by blood. But we were her own in every true sense. We were his, by blood. But in no other sense.

I was not aware for so long of how she spared us, how she protected us. She shielded our bodies with hers, our souls with the strength of her will.

My sister, Macha, and I did not understand the peril in which we existed. As we matured, we came to know it was there. Though we were silent then, we have since shared our stories, one with the other.

Our tongues were loosed that day, finally on that day of my mother's last story. We could speak then, denounce our father. We could only do so because she had protected us, taught us, fed us with her strength, and then freed us.

At that time, we could only feel the unholy abandonment that her absence would have inflicted. How it would have crushed upon us. But then we knew.

He belittled her, privately, publicly. He knew that we grew in her strength, but also knew how to twist her words, her actions. He knew the peril he was facing if we were her daughters rather than his.

Biann! he raged at me. Macha! I didn't hear his words.

We abhorred her station, where he had put her, and were often in danger of acting toward her as he did. But always, I am not certain how, we both could again recognize him for what he was and what he was doing. More importantly, we recognized our mother again, our sustainer and protector, before we had gone too far.

And we grew strong. Our mother, though strong in will, compassionate and loving to us, her adopted daughters, physically appeared to be shrinking, as if his attitude and cruelty were whittling away at her. We watched in horror, uncertain how to help her. Silent to each other, not daring to stray out of certain boundaries for fear of our father, and fear of the truth.

I am, Biann, the youngest, and the end came when I was of a womanly age.

Only once before had I seen anything of such power. A storm of such magnitude, the wind and the sea rising up to stand in tall waves and crash the shore and smash the boats.

But this power was silent, making it all the more awful. Silent at first. When I told her of the changes in me, she smiled serenely. At last, were the words she murmured.

Our father arrived with his usual cruel sneer and sharp words. My mother stood, gathered my sister and me to her sides, arms on our waists, and she grew larger. It was a fearful sight, awe-inspiring, growing taller like the sea's wave. I and my sister, for she told me so later, grew with her, fearful, anxious, and, yes, thrilled.

The wave crashed on our family life in his house, smashing all that we had known and understood. Our father, thunderstruck at our mother's words, her fiery spirit, her blistering power, said nothing, sank to the floor, struck dumb.

Then, all was silent again.

Where my mother had always followed him, head down, she now strode to the door and looked back at us. Fire was still in her eyes, though she appeared to be of normal stature again. Her voice was calm as moonbeams. Choose now, Macha, Biann, she said to us.

She walked out the door. We followed her, my sister and I.

We still do, in a sense, though she has departed from this life. Moon and sea, we are like her, and we would choose no other way to be.

Lucidity  1

He had come into our lives as a guest of a friend. My father did as was expected of him and treated him as a friend, for that is what we do—though he knew him not at all before the day he arrived at our door.

This Stranger—as I still call him to this day though not in my father's presence—no, we do not speak of him—was not gracious.

From that moment when he first stepped into our home, he acted as if he was entitled to all. Later, the man who introduced him tried valiantly to apologize, embarrassed beyond words. That man was shamed. He did not return to our family home for many months, though my father would have made him welcome despite all.

But the Stranger—he was entitled to my father's food and hospitality, and he preyed on my father's good nature and excellent manners.

Then, he took free reign of my father's employees. And attempted to take our family's wealth, one coin, one hospitality, one day at a time.

An overnight stay turned into days, and then weeks.

He spoke at every meal. He spoke foolishly and overlong. He stated random opinions only to set bait for others. To pick fights. To admonish and berate, belittle and frustrate.

Some considered him holy, worthy of respect. One other acquaintance proclaimed this man, this Stranger, the best extemporaneous speaker he'd ever heard in this age.

But I knew.

This Stranger overspoke, overate, drank too much wine, and overstayed.

Then he, in all his delusion of entitlement to all that was my father's house and household, attempted to take liberties with my sister—younger than I by three years, barely a woman herself. I entered the room as she was trying to wrench herself from his grasp. Tem! My sister cried to me, Tem! I'm so ashamed, she sobbed.

And then she fled, tears streaming down her face, gulping for air, red-faced and mortified.

At first taken aback, the Stranger regained composure quickly. He casually combed his beard, pretending to be irritated with me. Then, with a knowing wink, he departed from the room.

I waited.

At the evening meal, my sister was absent. I had seen to that. As this Stranger made ready to help himself to wine, bread, and meat, I stood.

My father, struck by my audacity and strangeness, said nothing. His eyes did not even show a paternal warning, so surprised was he.

I fixed my eyes upon the Stranger. This apparently was his first inkling of any danger to his position.

Stranger, I proclaimed. I am Tem, my father's daughter, my sister's friend. My voice was strong and steady, though I could feel fear flickering in my breast. Do you not know that you were not invited here and that you are not welcome?

I did not sit down or lower my eyes, though I was sorely tempted to do so.

Had he breath, I am certain he would have blustered and then denounced me. But he seemed to me, in that strange moment, to be a boat with flagging sail, stranded without wind. Useless. Impotent.

The room was full of people, but it had never been so quiet.

Strange man, I finally said, slowly and deliberately, you take too many liberties.

I looked then pointedly at my father. He stood up, gazed at me for a moment. As his face grew red with rage, his demeanor remained calm. To the surprise of all—including me—he turned to that man.

Strange man, leave my house.

The Stranger began blustering and there was a time of some pandemonium. He left. All guests left, embarrassed and gossiping.

For some time, our family ate alone—whether due to being ostracized or not being invited, I did not know or care.

In time, life returned to a sense of normalcy and our house was once again known for its hospitality. And, of course, many came because they were curious about my father's Brazen Daughter.

We never spoke of it.

Lucidity  2

I was so young.

I felt such shame for years and years.

Let me tell you. Let me tell you so that you will know. Perhaps you will not then make the same mistake? Only listen.

I heard this one man speak, and it seemed to me he spoke with such clarity. And feeling. He started softly and built up passionately. His words struck me as a truth I had been seeking for all time.

I went to hear him again and again. I began to speak in my own way, when with my family and my friends—with the same certainty. I told them all the ways in which they were wrong and deceitful and much worse. Much worse things I told them. Accused.

Accusation after accusation.

At first, they listened and tried to speak their own truths. Olansi, they said, hear us. Then they argued. Then they ignored.

This distressed me.

As I grew to know this speaker, we had long discussions and he said it was a part of my journey. He comforted me, and yet admonished me when it appeared I did not feel strong.

Olansi, he said, hear me.

So, I listened.

And, so, I persisted, my voice eventually becoming more strident and my words bitingly cruel.

And as they all walked away from me, and the way I had chosen, I felt abandoned and triumphant. Hadn't he told me? Hadn't he said, Olansi, you will face such trials? That even my family would turn their backs on me because I followed truth? Didn't that save me, that they had walked away, scorned me, rejected me?

All because I knew all, I knew the only truth there was.

I was there, with him and his other followers, when my mother came to find me. I could tell by the Preacher's face that he was not pleased. He said nothing at first, as she began to plead with me to come home.

Olansi, she said, hear me.

Then he began to speak. See? His voice blared. Do you see now? He wasn't speaking to me, but to all the followers. Do you see how they are, these unbelievers? Do you?

Within moments several people had risen to their feet and one had my mother's wrist and another a handful of her skirt, and another hand reached for her hair.

Quite suddenly I was not so young and not so certain—and quite alive. I sprang to my mother's side. They fell away from her.

Do not touch her, I breathed. Do not, I hissed.

The speaker still looked triumphant, and bitter. I will never forget that look.

I gently took my mother's arm, and we walked away.

My mother's fright gave way to relief, and she took my arm.

Olansi, I said to myself, learn the lesson.

Do you see? Do not trust completely anyone who proclaims to be so very certain of anything. They are selling something—and perhaps all it is, is their own bitterness, shame, disappointment, and fear. Fear.

Be careful. Be wise. Be at least a little uncertain.

Kin  1

Limma made her way slowly along the street, stepping carefully and slowly, moving soundlessly through the noisy crowd. When she was buffeted or pushed, her face grew quieter and haughtier. She stood even taller. People who noticed her approach stood back, not quite meeting her eyes, muttering she could only guess what kinds of superstitions, blasphemous phrases, and bitter words.

When she was noticed and when the bodies and eyes avoided her, when the voices quieted to mumbles or silence, Limma knew pride. She did her best to continue without anyone being able to point to her pride, without anyone noticing it.

Though she walked this way almost every day at this time to worship in the temple, she recognized no one. It would have been beneath her to actually recall a face or know a voice.

They, however, she noted with a silent glee, recognized her.

Back and forth each day, Limma walked, at first jostled and then avoided.

In the house, the one she shared with her sisters in faith, she was hardly noticed. She was younger, newer, expected to take on the most arduous tasks, the most humble jobs. But here, out here, she was set apart, above.

She often chastised herself at the place of worship, for her mind wandered as she imagined and anticipated the walk back to her abode.

We do not mix, she had been instructed from her earliest days among them. Serve, the older ones said, without touching, without contamination. It had surprised her and even upset her at first.

Then Limma grew accustomed to it, and learned to relish the separateness.

One day, during this walk of pride, a pair of eyes caught hers and they did not avoid. They gazed at her, bright and large, shining from a mud-smudged face. But she did not see that, nor that the child was clad in rags, barely covering her though the wind was chill. No, she noticed the eyes.

She almost stumbled, but then caught herself. Quickly, she recovered and strode with hard steps toward the temple, not looking back. She did not dare to. The raggedy child's gaze rested on her back, she knew it.

For some time, those eyes stayed with Limma. She tried and eventually succeeded in dismissing them. The way back seemed almost dangerous, but she did not slip again. She forced herself to walk as slowly and purposefully as she usually did. Gaze above the crowd.

Several days passed, and she forgot. Then the eyes were there again, large and shining, the gaze unflinching.

This time she stopped right in mid-stride. She had not intended to. She tried to force herself to go on, as she had before. Since that did not seem possible, she forced herself to stare back at those eyes, and then take in the rest of the figure.

Disgusting. Dirty. Quite obviously a child of the street, no doubt offspring of one of those flesh-peddling women that were about. Limma's mouth screwed up in disgust. Still the child stared.

Then, she noticed that others stared, but they were staring at her and not the child. She drew herself up and continued on her way, haughtily, but all the way wanting to look back at the child to see if she followed this holy figure with those eyes. She kept a tight rein on her compulsion and her eyes aimed forward.

The next time, she drew close to the child without appearing to notice her. She quickly shoved a cloth containing bread into the muddy little palm and continued toward the temple.

The joy she felt in worship was like that which she had felt as a girl, back when she had first considered this holy life as a calling.

Strangely, she thought, strangely this happens. Will I feel more joy, more intensely, if I give her meat? The thought almost made her laugh out loud. Quickly, she muttered the words of prayer that she knew so well, to cover her mood and near outburst. But the prayer words were simply recited; she did not think of them. Only the joy.

Always now she walked her path with a bit of food, something she could conceal and quickly deliver. Every day now the child was there. Every day she came closer to meeting those eyes.

The day their eyes did meet, she stopped again as she had on that other day. The child had evidently attempted to wash, and her heart was deeply touched at the thought. Limma smiled at the child. The child did not smile back at first, but those eyes shone back at her. Joy. She smiled still. Then she took the child's hand, and they began to walk together, away from the temple.

She did not notice any people gossiping, though she did see some of their faces and believed she saw their smiles.

She smiled still.

Kin  2

I looked for her for so long, waited for her.

In the deepest, darkest forest. Calling her name though afraid my voice alerted the hungry beasts that lived there. I called, again and again.

I trudged through desert sands, squinting against the blistering brightness, trudging on when I thought I could not anymore.

I waited by streams, hoping the song of the water would lure her there. I was not comforted by the sound. Eventually I moved on.

At times, I left off searching. I grew tired, but so very restless still. I spent my time among others, raising cup after cup of wine, raising my voice, trying to still the restlessness, silence the call to search, to keep on searching.

Other times I withdrew, did not know the passing of day into night, week into week, lost for some time, immobile.

But to searching I returned.

It took me to places frightening and others strange and beautiful. Into dark caverns, onto sunny hilltops. I plunged into the depths of cold lakes.

I longed for her. I cried. I screamed. I mourned.

I dreamt of her. I often awoke, screaming, feeling those beasts in that dark forest, gnawing on my bones, dragging her into the undergrowth. Saw her plunging into the lake, falling beneath the ice, crying to me, Aquana, Aquana, save me.

I was frozen on the shore.

Then, one strange warm morning, after I slept a dreamless sleep, I felt a warmth in my breast spreading outward to my limbs. Even before I opened my eyes, I knew this was no dream, no illusion. I thought when this moment happened I would cry, faint, something. Instead, I spoke simple words, with my eyes still closed,

I am Aquana. I searched for you.

I was right here.

I should not have sent you away.

I never left.

I nearly gave up.

I did not give up.

I waited.

I waited with you.

I opened my eyes then. The sun shone warmly on my skin, echoing the warmth and light I felt inside.

My daughter.

My mother.

My self.

Allegiance  1

I had been taught well, by father, brother, and mother. I was calm in demeanor, humble and obedient.

That was the face I was taught to show and I learned well.

And when the time came, I was shown before a select set of men, one at a time. I cooked a meal for each, served it, sat close by, anticipating needs as each man ate, laughed, bartered, leered at servant girls.

Each test I was more than adequate to pass. As I said, I learned well. My mother said, Dorpra, your father and brother are proud. I did not see it. I did not hear it from them. Only through others did I hear that now it was only a matter of who my father would choose for me. I believe he asked my mother her views, but she had not met most of the men. She deferred to him.

Malle, my brother, at first seemed unconcerned. He was quite proud that he was old enough now for my father to ask his views. He was careful in answering. Father's questions were often biased for either outright agreement or to instigate argument and debate.

But then I could tell my brother grew indifferent, or appeared to do so.

I was not indifferent, but I had learned well to put on that face.

Not one of these suitors looked at me in any way that I liked. Some leered, some sniffed their indifference, appearing to be courting my father—a powerful man—rather than me. Some looked cruel.

I prayed. I tried to pray for guidance, but often slipped into prayers for salvation, escape from these terms of courtship and forced partnership.

I could not turn to my mother. Unhappy woman, the face she had donned—of meekness and obedience—had long since hardened; it could no longer be doffed.

I turned to scripture. I grew even more unsettled, for it seemed to me—with my limited education—that I was to be treated more fairly than this, that I truly had a voice that was to be heard. The scriptures even spoke of love and desire—that which can be between two people without either being enslaved by the other. It shocked me and thrilled me. And confused me.

Had my mother ever read this? I became convinced that she had not.

My eyes began to be opened. I paid more attention to everything around me.

I could see my own brother's face of obedience—although a different kind of obedience—slip now and then. Malle struggled to show the indifference of the male heir in considering his sister's plight.

I came to know, too, that my brother loved. He was in love. He, too, had been attending his own dinners at a house where a daughter resided with her father and sisters. I was scandalized to learn they had actually met—my brother and this daughter of that household—outside the watching eyes of both families.

And I came to know that this young woman was promised to another.

I mourned for Malle. I mourned on his behalf.

My father grew smug. I feared he had made his choice for me. It baffled and frightened me. I knew of no one I wanted.

As I began to grow desperate, I tried to find a means of escaping this slavery—that is how I came to look upon it. Just then, Malle approached me. In his most arrogant tone, he said, Dorpra, make ready for a journey.

Indeed? I humbly asked. And asked no more.

He did not explain, until that evening after dinner. All guests had gone and I was helping remove soiled linens and dishes.

Father, I think it will be good for Dorpra. We go to visit our Aunt, to see her before she leaves.

My aunt and her husband were leaving for a far country in a matter of a few weeks.

It is right, my brother continued, that we should see her and my Uncle before they go. After all, they would not be able to come back for any festivities.

There it was. My father, it was clear, had made his decision.

I grew very still inside.

Malle waited as my father picked gingerly at some sweets remaining on his plate. Finally, he nodded. It is good, he said. Everything can wait for your return.

We left the following morning. My mother had helped me pack for a few days' journey.

It took much of the day to reach the city where my Aunt currently resided. As we approached, my brother broke his silence.

My sister, he said softly, dear Dorpra. His voice was softer than I had heard in years. My eyes grew moist, for that was how he used to speak to me when we were younger. And happier.

My sister, he said again, and finally looked at me. To our Aunt you go. She leaves on the morrow.

It was hard for me to conceal my surprise, but I said nothing. Yet I knew my eyes and the pink in my cheeks betrayed the questions that sprang into my mind.

Go with her. Be free of this place. Aunt knows. She will take you. She knows the situation.

My breathing grew rapid and then slowed again. He noticed.

Do you love any of those men, dear sister, he stated bitterly. It was not a question. In any other situation, with any other man, I would have lowered my head and said nothing. As I had been taught to do. But I fixed my eyes on his.

No, Malle, dear brother. I do not.

He nodded, fully satisfied, and still sad.

Then go with Aunt.

But… I started. I wanted to ask so many questions. What would he say to father? To mother? What…

He shook his head before I could form the words to speak them. Just go, he said quietly. I do not know when I will see you again.

I touched his hand, briefly. He looked at me in surprise.

Thank you, Malle. I do not know how else to say it.

Suddenly, he laughed. His eyes lit up. The old, playful laugh I had not heard in so long.

One of us should be free, he said.

Allegiance  2

I had five sisters. We were our parents' pride and joy. They were prouder of us, I know, than our grand house, or many servants, and our fine clothing and food.

The prized us above all.

They gave us all we could ask. When we demanded, they yielded.

We grew quite vain, all of us. Vain and proud. Haughty. I believe we were quite unbearable beings.

We were generally good to each other and, most of the time, to our parents. I cannot boast that we were good to anyone else.

I, Innilla, was the youngest but one. I was so very proud of my youngest sister. She was so beautiful, yet somehow less vain than the rest of us.

At a young age, just barely into womanhood, she sickened with a mysterious fever. Within a few days, she died.

We were devastated. Shocked.

My father and mother staged a grand funeral. Many mourners attended. We dressed in dark colors, mourning and attempting to comfort each other. It was so hard in such a public place. I believe my sister would have hated the pomp and splendor of that occasion. For reasons I did not understand, my parents and my sisters took comfort in it. I did not, and I did not see how they could.

Looking back now I can recall the moment when we, as a mourning cortege, passed out of our gates moving toward the burial ground. Though often beset with weeping in those hours, in that moment I was dry-eyed.

It was but a moment—a mere glimpse. I saw a small group of mourners, dressed in threadbare clothes, some in rags, carrying a girl's body. Though I could not see her for the shroud, it was clear to me she had been poor, as were her family and friends. Her people carried and escorted her body.

In that moment, I hated the pomp of our ceremony and dress. Once again, I became convinced that my dead sister would have hated it, too. This was not based on any knowledge or fact, only a feeling of that moment

Innilla, I could almost hear her say. Innilla.

Since that day, many years ago now, I have often dreamt the same dream. In it, my beloved dead sister comes to me. Her sweet face peers out of that dark and shabby shroud, as if she had been the poverty-stricken young woman who had been carried and buried on that same day.

She says nothing in the dream.

I have tried to tell my sisters of this dream. They listened patiently at first, but over the years have shushed me, shouted at me, entreated me not to continue. No, Innilla, stop.

My parents mourned and were never the same. My sisters somehow moved past this sorrow, though they were forever touched by it as well.

I left my family a few years later, having decided to join a religious order devoted to serving others, especially the poor. My sisters were shocked, as were mother and father. They have never understood. It was not something I could explain to them.

How I wish I could tell them of my younger sister living in me. How I wish I could explain how that dream at first haunted me, frightened me, and condemned me. Now, when she comes, she is a friend, a confidant. She no longer wears a shroud—that horrible shabby cloth. I can tell that her clothes are not rich and fine, but she is no longer shrouded. To me, she is not dead. How can I explain that?

I cannot.

I smile when I awaken. And I go back to my work.

Outsider  1

They come to me, Ropensa, those young women, with a slight arrogance borne of their station or their prospects. They are not pompous. Merely inexperienced.

They come to me so that they can learn. Learn from this older woman in her mid-years with grown children, and a husband long gone. This is the type of woman to teach these growing, inexperienced girls.

I teach them languages, and I see in several a real aptitude for numerous languages. I also teach them weaving and the arts of dyeing and spinning the wool into yarns.

They listen and learn at their ever-varying levels of skill and interest.

I am somewhat outcast, being the teacher. One of these girls is outcast because her people are not of the majority in this area, by race and religion. She struggles valiantly with the tasks I set for her. She shows a particular aptitude for languages. She is often alone, as I am.

I am to keep aloof, so I do. Yet I find ways to encourage her without being seen to do so. But she knows. She was afraid at first, but now is stronger.

The years pass and she is more accepted by her fellow students, who don't appear to know that they once shut her out. As she grows in years and her circle of companions grows, she moves away from me. It is subtle. I do not follow. I miss her, but I do not attempt to follow her path.

At the proper times, new students come and the older ones go. Off to live their own lives. When they go, they joyfully tell me good-bye. A few seem to have some passing sadness, as if they dimly realize and regret that they will not come here again—a place where they have lived and learned, and cried and laughed, for so many years. A very few even seem to notice me, and come to me to say a quiet farewell.

Ropensa, they say at the end, when they never said my name before.

When it comes time for her, my little former outcast, to carry her bags out, she looks at me. It appears to me that she remembers all. A momentary look passes between us, perhaps with some fondness and gratitude. It is hard to say.

Since then, I have relived that moment. I have never been able to picture her in my mind as a grown woman. She is to me as she was that day.

I am old and less able now. I teach only a little now.

One day, a woman in her mid-years, beautiful and grave, comes to me. She offers herself as teacher to these girls—and my caretaker. When she finishes her request, I ask her why.

Because, she says, someone once taught me and taught me the value of teaching. Of being taught. And she asked nothing of me or any of the others. I had nothing to give then. I might now.

As she speaks these words, I know her.

So many I tried to teach, I say softly.

She smiles that grave smile I knew so well from so long ago. You taught well, she says. And one has returned, Ropensa.

I look away as I speak. My eyes, always dry, are not dry now.

I always wondered… how I did. What they turned out like. What you…

She continues to smile, and there is warmth in the gravity. We have time. I will tell you all. Many stories. We will share, as we once did.

I smile, lonely no more.

Outsider  2

She stared at me, her eyes narrowing. I know you, she said. It was strange to me that a voice could be so flat and cold and so angry at the same time.

I gazed at her, letting my usually busy hands go still.

I do not know you, I replied.

Her cheeks flushed slightly as she set her jaw. Then she went pale again. I let the silence lengthen, still gazing at her. No, her face was not familiar to me. She was younger than I by 20 years, I guessed.

Let me make you some tea, I said. I began the preparations even as I spoke.

Her voice was tight. Tea? You offer me tea, Xana?

I offer you tea, I said. And a story.

As I continued preparations I was aware that she still stood there, not sitting down. I nodded to a chair. She remained standing. I set out cups and, when the water boiled, I spooned the leaves into the cups and poured the water.

Let it sit for a moment, I instructed as I sat down. She remained standing. She did not step nearer to the table or touch the cup.

Usually I felt a constant flutter inside me and could only master it by remaining busy. Now the flutter was strangely still. That is how I knew it was right to tell the story.

I have been told, I said, there was a time when my actions were evil. I caused pain. I ruined lives and families. Apparently, I had that power and I used it.

She remained where she was. I sipped my tea, not really tasting it. I knew that I had her attention, though I did not look at her. Those narrowed eyes were on me, I knew. I nodded, staring into my cup.

No, these are not excuses I am telling you. My actions were horrid. I betrayed people. My husband, my family. My sister.

I continued. This is what I have been told.

I seduced my sister's husband, when I grew tired of my own. When it was clear I could be discovered, I evidently did my best to make it appear that she had betrayed me with my husband. My plan worked.

Her own husband, my lover, convinced her that her only honorable option was suicide. She wept and then complied.

I became her children's guardian. I sent them away to be schooled and raised by others. There were three—two girls and a boy. They were not cared for. The boy and a girl died. Disease or neglect. I do not know.

The other girl disappeared.

I looked up at her, meeting her eyes for the first time since I had told her I didn't know her.

That is what I've been told, I said.

Her eyes were wide, not narrowed. Slowly she moved toward the table and sat down. She did not touch the tea.

What you have been told, Xana, she repeated, her voice quiet, her jaw still set.

What I have been told. Several years ago, the people who run this place found me by the side of the road just outside this town. I was unconscious. They brought me here, certain I would die. They nursed me back to life.

They do not know, nor do I, what I was doing in that place. I remember nothing before… just waking in their presence, with all these children around me.

Perhaps, I said, Xana was my name. But it is not now.

I allowed my eyes to wander to take in the room again, then dwelling on the fire in the fireplace. Then I looked at her again.

The woman's face had softened. She was quite pretty, really. She appeared to be the right age. I pondered. Does she have my sister's face?

I have been told many things about who I was. I leaned forward, wanting her to understand, but not expecting her to.

I do not know why I have been so blessed with no memory. And good work to do.

Blessed? The young woman said sharply.

I nodded, leaning back in my chair. Blessed. I did such things. Then, I shook my head. I count it as blessing to not remember that. Otherwise, how could I do other than die myself? I help care for these orphans.

You want redemption. The voice was soft.

Perhaps. Perhaps I do.

Her face was strong again, but anger was not there.

I know the Divine is in the moment, only in the moment, I said, not looking at her. If she was to scoff and berate me, I thought, it would be now. I prayed for the strength to take it.

Nothing but silence.

Finally, I said, I have been blessed with no memory of that time so that I cannot look back and dwell on the past. I must be in the moment.

It is a blessing, she said. One you do not deserve.

So I have been told.

She stood. I let my eyes rest on her hands, then raised them to meet her eyes.

You will remember me now? From this moment?

I will, I replied. Go, I said silently, be at peace.

She nodded. And then she was gone.

I went back to work.

Equity  1

They brought her to me, and I studied her. Eyes downcast, spine straight, lips set in a thin line. Defiance oozed from her, and I did not like it.

I took a deep, silent breath.

You know the accusation, I prompted.

She looked up then, which surprised me. She hadn't done that before, looked straight at me. Her eyes were dark and distant. After a long pause, she spoke, never once breaking our gaze.

I do, she said softly, her voice melodious. Then, almost shyly, she lowered her gaze to the floor again.

I felt a little unsettled. It was strange. Coming into this, I was quite sure what I would say and do.

Keeping a steady gaze and a strong but stern expression on my face, I allowed myself a moment or two to assess. The pause grew longer. People started to fidget, so I cast my eyes around the room, above their heads. The fidgeting stopped and the deep silence was restored.

I returned my gaze to her. She had not moved. A small strand of hair had escaped the knot at the back of her head, and it looked like it was tickling her check. But she did not move.

Finally, I recalled my next move. I stretched my fingers and said, in my best judicial and yet motherly tone, I grow tired of coming back to this same situation.

No response.

Don't you? I prompted, suddenly feeling irritated with her stone-like stance.

Once again, rather quickly this time, she looked up at me.

I do.

Her eyes focused again on the floor.

Have you nothing more to say than that? I had lost all maternal feeling, if that had been there at all. My words were sharp.

Nothing more than has been said before, Teliope, she said distinctly, enunciating each syllable. I did not do what they say. No one has proved anything. What is mine should be returned to me.

This last part came out in short clipped statements, as if by rote. The eyes stayed downcast. The voice was, at the end, tired and without inflection.

Hopeless. That is the word that came to me. I was startled, but refused to show it.

Have you any witnesses? The question came out of my mouth, surprising me more than everyone else in the room. Fidgeting and whispers ensued for a moment, and then all was silent again.

Witnesses to my innocence? She asked softly, eyes circling the room for the first time. Finally, those dark pupils focused on me. No, Teliope.

I was supposed to tell her the consequences. The words You are banished… rose to my tongue, but my lips did not open. Her eyes were still upon me. There was anger there, but resignation, too.

She had fought by not fighting. Denied the accusations without accusing in return. Offered no proof, but also had not had anything truly proved against her.

The thought was new to me, and made my head hurt. Irritation burned my eyes. I glared at her. The room was silent as a tomb, the eyes staring at me reminded me of so many shocked corpses.

I turned my head ever so slightly and caught the wide open and angry eyes of one of her accusers.

You, I said. Step forward.

Yes, Teliope. He shuffled toward me a few steps, eyes still angry but his facial expression wary.

Who are your witnesses? I demanded, making my tone sound bored.

His jaw moved and then his lips, but no sound came out at first. I narrowed my eyes at him. He croaked, No one.

No witnesses?

He shook his head, not even trusting his voice to speak again.

Stand back, I ordered with contempt, and his shoulders dropped as he slid back to the comfort of the other bodies in the room.

I located the other accuser, who appeared to be both trying to hide and unable to keep her eyes off the proceedings.

You, step forward.

She slowly moved through the crowd, throwing a sharp glance at the first accuser, who determinedly avoided her gaze. Then her eyes slid down.

Witnesses?

She didn't speak, and then shook her head in the negative.

I pursed my lips, and she looked up. Fear was there in her eyes, vying with the hatred she obviously felt. I almost smiled, or bared my teeth, at her.

Proof? The word was sharp, scathing.

She blinked in fright and whispered, No, Teliope.

I turned back to the first accuser. Forward.

He shuffled toward me again.

You will return her possessions to her, I announced proudly, thrilled at my own sense of right. You will not approach her again for any reason.

The crowd shifted in place. I leaned back and studied them, letting a slight smile appear. The accusers trembled.

I flipped my hand. Your accusations are dismissed, I announced.

I looked at the crowd. I was suddenly tired of the entire spectacle. I was tired of all of them.

You are free to go, I said to the accused, looking directly into her eyes.

I stood up. Her eyes followed mine. They were unreadable.

As I left I knew her eyes and others' would follow me out. I moved slowly, though I truly wanted to leave quickly. I shrugged a little and smiled when the door closed behind me.

She might make a good Arbiter.

Equity  2

Some would call me fortunate. I am the recipient of a wealth of unsolicited advice and well-intentioned reproof.

Guidance.

Sermons governing how I should act. What I should say. The feelings and thoughts I should have and should not have.

Orders I am to follow.

A mask I should wear, especially when I do not want to do so.

Time and again, I have acquiesced. I have trodden down, dismissed, rejected my own thoughts and feelings and, what's more, my own knowledge. The wisdom I have gained.

For so many years I have allowed myself to be pushed, pulled, bullied, punished, led, dragged. By parents, husband, children, siblings, neighbors, members of the community.

And all of this purchased at a price.

For I have known, instinctively, that to stand up for myself—to speak out, to walk away from parents, spouse, family, community—is to be alone.

Yet, am I not already alone? Knowing that? That I cannot believe what they believe, use the words they would have me use, feel only what they would have me feel, see only what they see, hear and heed only their views, think only as they would have me think.

Does that not isolate me?

My mother said to me when I was a child, Yonie, be yourself and they will like you. What she should have said is—and I know it now—Yonie, be yourself whether or not they like you.

Or respect you.

Befriend you.

Harm you.

Reject you.

Banish you.

I am being myself now. I stand up in their midst. They are shocked because I have been so acquiescent and now I am defiant. They raise their voices, gesture with fists.

I walk away.

I am alone. At first.

I look up, brushing tears from my cheeks. The woman in front of me seems familiar to me, and yet… she smiles. As I do. She extends her hands. As I do. We clasp hands.

Come, Yonie, she says. We've been waiting for you.

Illumination  1

I didn't trust her.

She may have taken me in and fed me when I was starving. It was temporary. I had to convince myself of that. Otherwise, I'd go crazy.

I remembered, vividly, the reds and oranges as my father muttered that he loved me, caressed me, threw me out of his house, screaming with rage. That's how I saw it—all of it—in red and orange. Blood red. The pasty orange of a corpse's changing face, just before it turns gray. Pearna, ravished and banished by her father.

I remembered vividly my first caretaker's assurances and his uninvited overtures. The rusty color of disgust, the dull brown of acquiescing, the gray and then black of losing consciousness. Gray clouds building and storming, over and over again.

Her colors were blue and green. But I eyed them suspiciously. It was too good. That other woman had appeared to be all blues, too. But her demands had turned into stormy purple and red rages—so like my father's that it surprised me.

No, I told myself, this woman's greens and blues would dissipate, intensify to some unearthly hue. Some change would happen.

But I take the food she offers, sleep on this blanket she gave me, though always alert to changing colors.

Slowly, it dawned on me that it had been days since I'd dropped exhausted and ill on her doorstep. Days on days. I still was wary of her, not even gazing directly at her, nor at her subtly changing green, blue, aqua, teal shadows and lights.

I had grown stronger. I could feel it. I'd begun to help out where I could, trying to find a time to plan my next move, but always feeling a dull red cloud on the edges. Encroaching.

Thank you for your help, Pearna, I dimly heard, the voice coming from beyond the red cloud. I felt a happy warmth, but the cloud was still there.

Every day, more blood red, sick orange, dull gray faces, bodies, souls walked through the door. She—and then we—soothed, fed, clothed them, bundled them into blankets, held them when the red screams and rusty sobs came and went.

This morning, just now, it is quieter. I find myself staring at her, feeling a rosy pink color and a swirling summer green drift in and out of my sight, but knowing those are my colors, not hers.

She looks at me, having felt my gaze on her. Yes, Pearna? she asks, ready for the question. I can't form it, other than this.

Why?

She looks around at the bodies and souls around us. All seems to go quiet, though I think it is just the rush of blue light surrounding her that fills and hushes the room. Then, for a popping moment, there is red, blood red, in her eyes. A memory. She looks straight at me, as the red fades away.

And then I knew. She had once been here as a recipient of food, blankets, and compassion. She nods, having said nothing, knowing that I know. She moves on to her next task.

I sit for a moment, absorbing the blue light that lingers, and then the scarlet colors of pain return in spots and clouds where people sit and lie, around the room.

I move to one, hold the woman's child, and coo to them both as I hold her mother's hand and soothe her. And I wonder, am I green? Or pink? To this woman and her child, am I a blue light?

I find comfort that I might be.

Illumination  2

It is heresy, he claimed.

It was difficult to hear such anger and hatred and not shrink from it. I found my voice, small though it was.

It is not, I replied softly.

Is that up to you to say, Suu'la? He thundered.

I looked up at him, unable to conceal my surprise. Yes, of course, I answered.

His face flushed. Even in the dimly lit, cold cell, I could tell. I shivered.

These people, he almost whispered, though I was certain all could hear him. These people assembled here. Do they not have more learning than you? Read the holy texts?

He waited. I did not know how to answer, because it had sounded like questions, and yet more like statements of fact. He looked smug and began to strut in front of me.

My knees hurt so much, but I pushed the pain aside and breathed deeply.

These learned people, he continued, they know more, have read and studied. Suu'la, you defy them. You show disrespect and speak these words as if they are truth. It is for these people to say what is heresy.

He stopped in front of me. I stared at him. Still I had heard no question, so I waited.

Evidently, he had expected some kind of verbal response.

The cold stone step dug into my knees. I noticed that I could no longer feel my feet.

It is heresy that she speaks, he finally said to those gathered in the cell, satisfaction in his voice. He drew breath and began to strut again, about to speak.

It is not, I said.

His body jerked to a stop. He sputtered, his words appearing to fall back into his open maw, ready to choke him.

Presumptuous! He panted and then began screaming. How can you presume? How can you spout such evil? How can you bring such harm, or try to, by stating such untruths?

It is true.

Blasphemer! He drew his face into a sour pucker, then leaned down. I felt his heavy breath on my cheek and smelled its sourness.

Repent.

One word, but it chilled me.

And then I began to grow warm. My legs, though numb and painful at the same time, bothered me not at all of a sudden. I smiled at him. He cringed and slunk away from me. I found my strong voice, as my eyes followed him.

How can I pretend I do not know? How can I keep silent when the truth forms on my lips? When the words come to me unbidden? How can I keep this hope, this life to myself?

He was silent. The room was silent around us, the air heavy.

I cannot, I stated simply. Then I let myself go silent.

I said no more, even as he ranted and raved. I withdrew my mind.

Some time later, I found myself on the floor of a different cell. It was dark. I could feel that it was cold, and yet the cold did not touch me.

Sister. A voice from a void beyond the cell door.

Yes.

Did they torture you?

I could tell the voice was frightened. I could not see the speaker. I knew that I did not recognize the voice, but I did recognize the pain in it.

No, I replied. And to myself, because I did not feel tortured.

I began to sing, thoughtfully forming the words and notes. An old tune my mother had taught me when I was much younger. The restless pacing in the next cell ceased, and her low melodious voice joined in. Fear subsided. I could hear other voices blending in. It was as if the very walls and stone floors joined in and we were comforted.

Remedy  1

She knew the hour had come. She called her children to her.

Her vast store of strength was waning. She did not mourn its loss, though she did wonder at its strangeness. How bereft she felt in a way. She had always had energy. But now a limited amount.

My dear children, Weshilana crooned, I am going to tell you a story.

The eyes that met hers were sad and attentive.

A woman had a small plot of land. On this plot she planted seeds of a certain kind. As the tiny plants grew, she noted one that was of a different type than she expected. Impatiently, she tore it out of the ground, roots and all, and tossed it aside. Without her noticing it, it took root again and grew slowly. At harvest time, it bore different fruit than the rest, but it was the best, most succulent fruit.

Weshilana paused for a moment, panting a little. She regained her breath, and proceeded.

A man discovered a spring of freshest water, fresher than the well he and his neighbors shared. He reasoned that water diverted from this spring would make his field grow more food than his neighbors' and that would result in more money, perhaps more prestige in his community. He diverted the rivulet from its natural course. Each week, however, he noted that the spring returned to its path, and his diverted stream dried up.

The spring's path was strong, Weshilana whispered.

The mother felt her strength ebbing even more. She smiled. It was almost time. One more story.

The daughter, she began, was not valued. Her parents placed her in a position of servitude. The sons were honored and spoiled. The first son fell into a dissolute lifestyle. He gambled and soon was in great debt. With that, he disappeared. The second son fared no better.

The mother paused to take a deep breath.

The second son. He was lazy and arrogant. He grew promiscuous and started a fight with a lover's husband. He was killed.

The third son labored for a time, but grew ever more irrational. He beat the servants, frightened his family; he ranted and raved. In madness, he grew ever more violent and the community rose up and took him away.

Through it all, the daughter labored—kept the house, treated all in the household fairly, kept the records, spent only what was necessary for the family's food and shelter. She was steady and wise. She kept hearth and home. When all others strayed, she stayed.

On her the family relied. She lived to a ripe, old age.

Weshilana sighed again, and continued to smile at her children. She wanted to ask them, all gathered around her, if they understood her stories.

Then, without asking, she knew they did. She was satisfied.

Remedy  2

Did you not preach to us of abstinence? Mecinne's tone was sober.

Gona remained silent. The interrogator waited for a moment for an answer. When he offered none, Mecinne looked down again at the paper, fingering the texture of the page as if she could feel the charges written upon it.

Did you, or did you not, admonish us for theft and thievery? she declared.

His anger stirred. He had told himself he would offer no answers. He would not lower himself to acknowledge their accusations. Though it took much of his fortitude, he did not do more than glare at her.

Her voice continued, as did the motion of her head, as she looked down to read the charge and then looked at Gona—with no real expectation—for an answer.

Did you not counsel us against disbelief?

This was too much for him. He flushed, though he tried to control himself.

I kept the laws, he declared in a loud voice, louder than he had intended. He forced himself to be silent again.

All the laws? Mecinne pursued.

He set his lips in a firm line and tried to stare her down, as if he was the accuser and she the accused. Her gaze was as flat as her voice had been. His gaze shifted, and he grew angrier at the weakness he perceived in himself.

Did you not state that we should not kill?

I did not! Gona blustered. His skin faded from red to a whitish-gray. Those nearest him wondered at the change. Might he collapse?

That other woman's face floated before him as it had appeared that first day. She had noticed him in his fine robes, had made sure he noticed her. Or, so he thought. So he wished to declare. He wished to accuse her, to reveal her wickedness.

Then he remembered the fear. Her eyes had widened. She had pleaded. It had excited him to a pitch he had never before experienced. How she fought him. How the forcing enraged and engorged him.

And, the passion spent, his passion, how dull her eyes were, how pasty her skin, the skin of her neck beneath his hands. How her voice had died as the life was strangled out of her. Her life. His hands.

The people noticed he had lifted his hands before his face, and made a small gasping sound.

Now they came to the second part of the ritual.

Did you break abstinence?

He said nothing, but in his mind Gona said, I did.

Did you steal?

Again, to himself, I did.

Did you not believe?

To himself, I do not know.

Did you break the laws?

He sighed, but again silently proclaimed, I did.

Did you kill?

Out loud now, I did.

Several people stirred. A murmur grew and faded in the room.

Mecinne stared at him. Then she said, Do you know the sentence?

I do.

Perception  1

What is it, my child? Why do you cry?

Ishka stared up at her father, at first unwilling to share the cause of her tears.

It's selfish, she admitted, shaking her head and wiping at her cheeks.

He handed her a small towel. Tell me, he encouraged her in a kind voice.

Our neighbors, Ishka began. Her tears dried as she wondered how to proceed, the skin tightening on her cheeks.

Have they hurt you? His voice was taut, on the edge of anger.

She looked quickly into his eyes and placed her hand on his. Oh no, father, nothing like that.

He relaxed. Good. Then, tell me.

She felt even more embarrassed, but cleared her throat to proceed. They have many things, she said. Many fine things.

Yes.

A very fine home. She almost stopped there, but continued. It would feel better if she said it all. A fine home, she continued, fine clothes. Fine food.

And the daughter of the house. She is your age?

Ishka nodded, a stubborn look on her face. Her own horse. Such fine dresses.

She fidgeted under his gaze. His eyes were profoundly sad.

Oh, father! I'm sorry. I told you it was selfish. I won't speak of it again.

Ah, my child, he sighed. He arose to look out the small window, staring out at the stone barrier that marked the end of his land and the start of his neighbor's.

I'm sorry, she repeated weakly.

No, no. I am glad you told me. It must be hard for you, to be so much in her presence and see such a difference in your… situations. He glanced back at her. Come here, daughter.

She rose. He drew her in front of him so she, too, could look out the window.

Note those stones.

Yes, father.

See how it is clear that several have fallen away.

Yes.

And you know that continues to occur.

Yes. She knew this well. It was often her father who repaired the wall, though it was really the neighbor's responsibility.

When our neighbor built that fence, he rushed through the job.

And where you have repaired it, she replied, it has remained in good shape.

Yes. Come, let us sit again.

He lit a candle, for it was getting dark in the little house.

That is how it is. You are old enough to know. Our neighbor… he paused. He did not wish to speak ill of anyone. He began again. In my view, he said, our neighbor has built his life and fortune that way. Quickly and unwisely. Tales are told and he himself has mentioned the enormity of his debt to others.

Ishka gasped.

And, you have your young man? He smiled at her.

She blushed. I do. She added quickly, Though she has many suitors.

Are they worthy men? Like the man you are to marry?

She pondered this. No, she admitted. Perhaps not.

He leaned forward to take both his daughter's hands in his. He was getting older, but his hands were still strong.

What your mother and I built here we did slowly, steadily. This is a sturdy, good life we live.

Yes.

You and your family will continue as we have done.

She felt proud and humbled at the same time.

We are rich, he said softly, almost to himself. His eyes were alight.

She beamed back at him. Yes, father.

His smile waned. And our neighbors. I fear their lives are much the same as that fence.

She rose. She walked to the front door, opened it, and walked out into the dusk. He sat waiting, surprised at her departure. After a few moments, she returned, clasping a small stone. She placed it on the sill of the window out of which they had both looked moments before. After a moment of contemplating it, she turned to look at her father. She smiled.

Lest I forget.

Perception  2

When Traul heard of his preaching, she listened with interest to the secondhand accounts, then shook her head a little in wonder. Then, she returned to gathering the soiled linens, washing and repairing them, and checking the stew.

His traveling brought him near her part of the village. In a startling move, she put her work aside for a time, to hear him speak with her own ears.

After a time, she left that gathering and returned to her place. Once again she began the next meal, cleaned up after the children, and went out to tend the small garden.

The preacher had heard of her ceaseless toil and of her leaving her duties to hear him speak. As he and his followers began to move on from that area, he asked where she lived. They guided him to her abode. He looked with great curiosity at the rambling old building.

What is this place? he asked.

He was told that it was Traul's house, inherited through many generations. They told of how she had begun to take in men, women, and children who had no other place to go. How she cooked and cleaned for them, treated them when they were ill, spent her inheritance on helping these people.

It is rumored that her inheritance cannot last forever, one follower told him.

Forever is inconsequential, he scoffed.

He strode up to the door. Traul answered his knock. She was surprised at his arrival, and stared at him and the many people crowding the street in front of her house.

You heard me speak, he declared, loudly. He wanted all to hear.

She nodded.

The end is coming, he stated.

That is what I heard you say, Traul admitted.

Your toil will not last forever, woman.

No one's toil lasts forever, preacher.

He stared at her. He was dumbfounded by her simple retort.

Finally he said, I am telling you of the end of times.

I heard you. I must go, preacher. The food might burn. I must check it.

She started to turn away.

But listen to me! Your toil can cease!

She stared back at him for a moment, and then again started to move away.

Your toil can cease, sister! He cried. For the end comes tomorrow, sister!

His declaration startled all, including himself. He regretted saying it the moment it left his lips. But he could not take it back now. He grew defiant.

The end comes tomorrow, he declared in a grand tone.

If that is so, it is so, Traul stated simply and again began to shut the door.

You show a lack of faith! He accused loudly, feeling a sort of desperation. He controlled his emotion and said grimly, Tomorrow, sister, tomorrow.

She shrugged. If it is to be, so be it. I still have tasks to do today.

She shut the door.

Power  1

Dearest sister,

You know of my trials. You know of my sorrows. You do not know all, but you will.

By now you have kissed my daughters in welcome. You are surprised to see them, but are joyful in their presence.

It is my sincerest hope they arrived without incident.

Please, sister, wait until after you send them to bed to read the rest of this letter.

You know that our elders have spoken many times to my husband about the violence he does to so many. He does so and has been reprimanded many times now.

Tonight is the end. I know it is. For last evening he harmed my oldest one. Note the bruises on her young legs.

It must end now. Tonight, I will prepare a simple meal. Then I will tell him his daughters are gone, never to return to live under his roof. I know what his reaction will be. He has threatened my life so many times.

Fear not, sister, for yourself! As you read this, so do the elders read a similar letter. And I have made our brother swear to protect all of you, which is why he is there with you and brought my daughters to you. He does not know all, else he would not have left me here. But I need to you to know, even as it is too late to save me.

The elders will come, sister, and my husband will not harm anyone any more.

Raise my daughters as your own, good sister! Tell them I love them so dearly!

My sister and brother, I love you, too.

I am so grateful my daughters are safe. I take comfort in knowing that I could do that much for them. They have suffered so.

Kiss them for me. Hug them for me. Hug them. Hold them.

With love,

Your Tiche

He stood for a time, simply watching her. Minbora was aware of his presence, but put the awareness aside to continue her prayers. Finally, she stood up stiffly, her knees sore and cold. Absently she rubbed at them, feeling the stiffness of her prison robe.

She knew the look on his face, very well indeed. That raw skepticism and something bordering on disdain.

Finally he said, You continue to pray.

It was against the rules to interact with prisoners, but they had long since ignored that rule. They spoke softly so no one would think it was anything other than a rat scratching.

I do, Minbora said. She was surprised at the subject.

You claim to believe in the same deity as those who brought you here.

There is but one deity, she replied, smiling at his bullying tone.

So you say.

To this she did not reply. She sat on her cot for a few moments, trying to guess the time of day. She was also trying not to feel the great hunger rumbling inside her. She almost felt faint with it.

It is foolishness, he badgered her.

She shrugged. No, it is not. And if it gives me comfort in this hour, is that not a good thing?

Foolish comfort.

Comfort is comfort.

He snorted. Out of the corner of his eyes, he peered at her as he pondered the exchange. Minbora was young and not overlay plain. Still he had not taken advantage, nor had any of the other guards. He was certain of it. He had always believed that type of behavior was undignified for any true soldier. Still, it happened with some prisoners. He knew this.

Yet not with this one. It was not to be contemplated with this one. He wondered what it was about her that defied mistreatment. And yet, here she was.

He had always wanted to ask her. Now that her time was drawing close, he decided to ask. Softly, he cleared his throat.

At the sound she returned from her memories, which she had been perusing in her mind and heart. She looked at him.

You are accused of sorcery, he said quickly, before he lost his nerve.

Yes. Minbora looked away.

What did you do?

She was silent for a long moment, then a long sigh escaped from her.

I heal.

He did not know how to respond. He was puzzled. How could that be such an offense, he wondered.

She walked a few steps toward him. Someone banged on the door. Always it startled him, even when he expected it. She never appears startled, he thought.

He opened the door. The other guard spoke a few words to him, and then put bread, water, and a bowl of broth on the floor. He left. The door was left open. He watched her as he was ordered to do.

She stood where she had been when the second guard arrived.

Go ahead and eat, he said gruffly, but not unkindly.

Your hand, she said. It hurts?

He was surprised. Yes, he said. A fight, he added, amused at his own tone, and the fact that the other man hurt more than he did.

Minbora said nothing more. He was disconcerted by the trembling in her voice and the look in her eyes.

As the other guard's footsteps drew close, she picked up the bread and sat down again on her cot. She did not eat.

The other man appeared. The first guard nodded at him and walked out the door. She was still sitting there, motionless, as the door closed. The guard shrugged and turned down the long corridor. It had been a day filled with boredom until his moments with her. He sighed.

As he reached to open the next door, he stopped and stared at his hand.

It didn't hurt anymore.

Accountability  1

Since then I can get no rest.

They brought her before me. I had already judged many cases by the time she stood in the room. My head ached and I was vehemently angry with the cries of the accused as well as the accusers. So many cases where the stories from each side had no common ground.

I can remember squeezing the bridge of my nose, scrunching my eyes, thinking that might do something for my pain. When I looked up, she was there in front of me. Several accusers stood facing me as well, their expressions ranging from rage to cold hate.

What is your name? I asked, my voice sounding gentler than I'd intended.

She did not answer, so her accusers answered for her.

Tunley, they said.

I remembered why this case had piqued my interest in the beginning. I had heard of her. She was the daughter of a wealthy man. She was constantly involving herself in others' disputes, attempting to help them seek a resolution. She flouted authority, it was said.

What is the accusation against Tunley? I asked. The voices of all the accusers rang out. I held up my hand and the noises subsided into irate murmurs. They threw each other glances filled with anger and exasperation.

You. I pointed at one of the men in front. He seemed to swell with pride and his eyes burned with excitement

She has not obeyed our laws, he said simply in a voice loud enough for all to hear. Murmurs ceased.

I stared at him. I had expected more.

He cleared his throat. And she speaks out against our laws… in clear defiance… of our laws.

To myself I thought, he does not even bother to provide an example. I continued to stare at him. Finally, I broke the gaze.

Do any of you have other charges to add? Before the din started up again, I held up my hand again. One at a time, I admonished.

The crowd shifted slightly, but no one stood forth. I remember thinking it was a waste of time and I would have to limit such encounters in the future. The pain in my head seemed almost to move about, but did not abate. I squinted against it.

No other charges, then. Very well, I said. I turned my attention to the accused and I studied her. She hardly looked like a troublemaker. True, she met my gaze with her own steady one, rather than looking down, demure, or even frightened.

What is your plea? I asked her.

Tunley said nothing.

Can you hear? I said petulantly.

She nodded once.

What is your plea?

She remained silent, eyes alert and gaze unwavering.

I do not recall how long I looked at her, trying to read her. The crowd began to shift again, with nervous feet and fidgeting hands.

I shook my head again a little to clear it.

What is your evidence? I asked, turning my attention to the accusers again.

One at a time they stood forth, railing against her and her words and actions. The accusations were grievous indeed, but incongruous with that still, silent figure before me.

The testimony, and that which the accusers assumed passed for evidence, seemed to last for hours. Finally, they were done. Strangely, they looked even angrier and more exasperated than when they first arrived.

I was at a loss. I did not believe they had proved anything against her. All just words.

Now, what do you say? I asked the accused. Still, Tunley said nothing at all.

Accusations with no evidence and no defense. Despite the weak case, my path was clear. Nevertheless, I felt a strange reluctance. So I tried again.

What do you say to these accusations? I proclaimed loudly, enunciating clearly, and deliberately, showing more anger than I felt.

She blinked at the sound of my voice, but then her gaze steadied again. She said nothing.

Deferred to a higher court, I announced abruptly, pounding my fist on the table before me. Take her away.

Some of the accusers smiled in satisfaction, mumbling to each other, She has no defense. Others looked dissatisfied with the entire proceeding.

It did not matter, I told myself. At least it was over, so it did not matter. Or, it should not have.

They led her out.

It was now out of my domain, I thought with relief.

Yet, why is it now, when I close my eyes to try to sleep, I am trapped in that silent gaze?

Accountability  2

Calmona moved slowly toward home, without any conscious effort.

So many witnesses, no one will speak of it.

She was dumbfounded and confused. Mere days ago, people had been excited and celebrating, speaking words of freedom, filled with joy. There had been dancing and singing.

She had watched all this with wonder. There seemed to be a center to the celebrations, someone Calmona only heard about but had never been able to catch sight of.

Without any trigger she had witnessed, the tide had turned. Violently. Voices were raised in anger and accusation. Dancing was replaced with hostile demonstrations, joy with rage. Fights broke out.

And, again, the center appeared to be this one person.

By the time she'd seen the woman, she was no more than a body with no spirit. The crowd had turned to a mob, and the mob had taken her life.

As her feet continued to guide her home, Calmona again felt the wonder, the dismay, and an underlying nausea. The feelings, from rage to fear, came and went like waves on the beach.

And now, all voices were silent. But, no, there were whispers. She had had to listen hard to hear, but then she did. She heard the stories, told with awe and wonder, of this now dead woman's work among the poor, the sick, and the outcast. From different areas, from people who did not know one another, the stories were amazingly consistent.

She listened harder. Behind closed doors, the voices grew less timid, less wary. Soon others asked her about the woman and the events, and she found herself telling the stories she'd heard.

Calmona thought of this with wonder and sorrow as she finally neared her home. She rested her forehead against the cool stone of the door frame. For a moment she stood there, and then she wept.

She cried for the life that was lost, and for the sorrow she felt about death and for never having met this woman.

When the tears subsided, Calmona entered her home. Methodically, with a lighter heart and a determination she had never before known, she placed clothing, food, and a flask of water into a bundle, and strapped the bundle on her back.

She left her house without looking back. New villages and new countries called to her. And she would go there. And she would tell the stories to any who would listen.

Certainty  1

I approach the mound where she is buried, and I weep. The ground is so raw, so newly turned, it makes my heart ache with sorrow about the extinguished body beneath this soil. I cannot keep from kneeling, picking up clods of earth, crumbling them in my tear-stained hands.

Why do you come here, child? I am not here.

I sort through her things, and I weep. Her robes and shoes. The scarf she often wore on her head, tied to keep her hair off her face as she worked. I finger the fabrics, wishing to feel the flesh of her arm beneath.

What do you seek here, my daughter?

I sit alone in the room she loved best, and I weep. The sunlight tries to reach me, but I have covered the windows. I try to picture her here, mending a shirt, sipping her tea, laughing at a passage I read to her.

I am not here, Folla.

My sister comes and forces her way into the gloom of the house. At first she tries to force me to stop crying. She speaks in a voice that is very nearly angry. I grasp her hands and pull her down, to sit with me. I see the pain she is trying to conceal. It is there in her eyes. I hold her hands, clutching them, feeling their warm flesh.

Folla, Folla, my sister murmurs.

Yes, child. I am here. Do you see me looking back at you?

I look up. I study my sister's eyes. Yes, I am here.

We stand and we walk. We go to her children. We watch them as they wonder what to do, how to act—struggling to be children filled with their natural joy, but sensing, though not understanding, the sorrows all around them. I coax my sister into a game with them.

Yes, I am here, Folla. Now, I believe you see me.

I visit the people she visited, nurse those she cared for. They are sorrowful, too, and express their condolences at my loss. And I for theirs. Sometimes we weep together. And they look at me with gratitude.

More than one tells me, in their own way, she never really left us.

That is true, I say.

She is here with us.

Certainty  2

You are here, my mother, my sister, my friend, my kin.

My Ansha.

I hear you in the whispering green trees under which you loved to walk. In the warm rain gently slapping the leaves in your lush garden.

I know you live in each seed you planted.

I see you in the objects you made with your own two hands, with love and compassion your only motives.

In the eyes of your loved ones, chosen family, and friends.

Ansha, I see you in the living.

You are there when I gaze at my own reflection. It is then I can see your smile.

Attend...

About the Author

Ann Greenseth has been a technical communication professional for more than 25 years. She holds a Bachelor's degree in Theatre and a Master's degree in English from Illinois State University. Her first love has always been writing fiction.

Ann lives in southeastern Wisconsin.

About *According to Lu*

How might celebrated spiritual texts differ if they had delved deeper into women's lives, or had even been authored by women? If sacred writings had illuminated and celebrated women's knowledge and experiences, in what diverse and creative ways might they have inspired others?

Ann Greenseth's novella, According to Lu, is a fictional example of such a text. Through its parables, letters, and narratives, the reader comes to know each storyteller, and witnesses how each works within their social and familial roles, or challenges them and questions expectations. These accounts testify to their spiritual and emotional lives—to their dreams, desires, actions, lessons, and trials.

The characters' sacred experiences and spiritual truths touch on varied themes including allegiance, passion, equity, power, rebirth, and more. Each theme and story recognizes the Sacred in the storyteller even as the characters themselves come to recognize and appreciate the Sacred in the women around them.

Lu, the collector of these narratives and "editor" of this anthology, sends the treasured compilation of testaments to Thea, her friend, kinswoman, and colleague. In doing so, Lu intends to share them not only with Thea, but with a much larger audience. It is their hope these accounts can serve to encourage women to share their stories and, in turn, comfort and inspire their friends, sisters, mothers, and daughters.

Made in USA - Kendallville, IN
1145519_9781734816907
08.06.2020 0851